Blaque Butterfly

When a Woman Evolves, Everything Burns

Mell B

Blaque Butterfly

Published independently by Mell B

Paperback ISBN: 979-8-9948739-1-5
eBook ISBN: 979-8-9948739-0-8
Hardcover ISBN: 979-8-9948739-2-2

Cover design by Mell B
Interior design by Mell B

First Edition

Printed in the United States of America

Prologue: The Betrayal in Chicago

Chicago never slept; it just changed shifts. The streets hummed low, a frequency only hustlers seemed tuned into. Engines idled too long. Sirens cried somewhere far enough to ignore. The wind sliced through the alley, sharp and impatient, like it knew what was coming. It was cold enough to make steel sweat, and the city reeked of desperation and diesel fumes.

R'Mell pulled her coat tighter and scanned the block. 79th and State looked quiet, too quiet for a Friday night. A black sedan rolled past the alley mouth again, slower this time. She wasn't new to fear, but this silence had a pulse, and it was offbeat. Dre was supposed to be here ten minutes ago. He's never late for a drop. She has called him twice, but her phone stays dark. Every second she was waiting felt like a setup breathing down her neck. She had doubts that Dre could get the money, but now that he's not answering, she may be right.

A flicker of headlights caught her eye. A black Escalade rolled up slowly, tires whispering over fresh snow. No plates. Tinted windows. She recognized that ride before it even stopped. Miguel Garcia. The name alone carried weight, the kind that could crush bones.

Dre had been hiding behind a dumpster a half block away. He watched R'Mell shivering and checking her phone. What he was really doing was looking for Miguel's men. Miguel never meets anyone alone. Dre's phone buzzed. He opened it and flipped it face down without looking. He knew it was R'Mell.

She swallowed hard, straightened her stance, and watched as Miguel stepped out of the shadows like he'd been there the whole time. Clean coat. Calm smile. Diamonds catching light, they didn't earn. He didn't rush. Men like Miguel never did. Power walked with them or limped behind.

"Where's Dre?" Miguel asked, smooth like honey over razor blades.

"On his way," R'Mell said, steadying her voice. "We good, Miguel. Dre will be here wit yo' money." Miguel smiled, but his eyes didn't move. "You sure about that? You always were smart, R'Mell. Smart women last longer."

R'Mell was confused and pissed off by his words. Before she could answer, Dre appeared from the alley with a duffel bag slung over his shoulder, grinning wide enough to sell a lie. "Miguel!" he said, arms out like they were old friends. "No need to be disrespectful."

Miguel eyed the bag. "You bring my money?"

"Of course," Dre said, setting it on the hood of R'Mell's car. "Count it, if you want."

Miguel motioned to one of his men, who met Dre halfway between the cars. The man kneeled and unzipped the bag. His face went pale. The bills looked right until he touched them, paper too light, ink too dull. Counterfeit.

The man looked back at Miguel. Miguel's smile died slow. "You trying to play me, Dre?"

R'Mell's stomach dropped. She cut her eyes at Dre because she'd told him not to do this, not with Miguel. Now her rage turned into fear. *This nigga finna get us killed,* she thought.

"Relax, man," Dre said, holding up his hands. "It's just business."

"Business?" Miguel's voice cracked the air. "You call tryin' ta pass fake money, TO ME, business?"

Miguel's guy stood up, and Dre took a step back, hand inching toward his waistband. R'Mell caught it too late. Miguel raised his arm, and all hell broke loose.

The first shot echoed off the buildings. Glass exploded. Dre ducked behind the car and returned fire. Miguel's men scattered behind their SUV, bullets flying like curses. R'Mell hit the ground, grabbed her Glock, and covered Dres's flank. Smoke clouded the street; screams turned to silence.

When the gunfire stopped, the air was thick with smoke and betrayal. Two of Miguel's men were down. Dres's shoulder bled through his jacket. R'Mell's hands trembled, not from fear but from rage.

She looked around. Miguel was gone. Vanished into the maze of Chicago's backstreets, but not before leaving his mark, a bullet hole inches from her head, a promise whispered in gunfire: *This ain't over.*

Dre groaned, clutching his wound. "We gotta go, Mell." She stood paralyzed for a moment, staring at the bodies cooling in the snow, the flashing red of faraway sirens, from the bridge overhead, reflecting off the wet pavement. The city had seen worse, but not from them, not until tonight. R'Mell is already planning what must come next.

She nodded once, jaw tight. "Yeah. We done here." R'Mell felt the night snap shut around her. Every exit, every lie, every future she'd imagined folded in on itself.

As sirens closed in, R'Mell wiped blood from her cheek and stood straighter. This wasn't over. It was just the beginning.

They left Chicago before sunrise, blood still drying on their hands, and a war following close behind. R'Mell didn't look back. But the ghosts did, and one of them had Miguel's face.

A New Beginning

It was after midnight, so no one knew what R'Mell and Dre were doing. The nightlife was going on as usual, so no one noticed. They packed light and loaded essential items in the back of the truck and the backseats. They were on their way to a better life, leaving behind life on the streets and its dangers. The lives R'Mell and Dre led were filled with drugs and money, both of which they inherited from their parents. Over the years, they both made some bad choices that could have gotten them and their families killed. R'Mell wanted to start a family with Dre. Bake sales and ballet recitals were a world away from the jagged reality of needles and drive-bys. A life where both of them can experience what genuine happiness and family feel like.

Riding through the hood was bittersweet for R'Mell. Children outside doin' flips on mattresses, the corner store dice game, and the grandparents outside sittin on their favorite porch rocking chairs, as she recalled. She grew up on the south side of Chicago. Her family was there. The rest of her living friends were there. She didn't want to leave, but things were hittin' too close to home. They were losing too many family members to drugs or murder. Dre didn't want to leave either. His ties to Chicago ran deep. He still had clients and connections that were depending on him. They would just have to turn to the next man for their needs. Dres' family adored him, especially his money. He helped the kids in his family. Adults should have their own hustle, he'd say. R'Mell and Dre have roots in Chicago, but their dream life is pushing them forward.

Passing through downtown, the city was still alive with people sitting on patio bars, the smell of pizzerias in the air, and the loud sounds of sirens speeding by. R'Mell could see the flashing lights of the Ferris wheel on the Navy Pier as they passed Buckingham Fountain in Grant Park. She suddenly started to daydream about when she met Dre for the first time at Navy Pier. Back then, Boyz to Men and roller-skating were her two favorite things. But when she decided to try something different, she met the love of her life at the roller rink. Her friends told her he looked like a bad boy, but R'Mell saw something familiar in Dre. He had the aura of someone who wouldn't let anyone stand in his way of what he wanted. That sent fire through her body that she was too young to understand, but would later excel in. The look in his eyes and the smile on his face when they walked past each other were unforgettable. They were young, and it was love at first sight. Meeting him changed her life forever. At the time, R'Mell was going through some growing pains, and her family didn't understand her at all. Dre was the only one who stayed with her. He understood what she was going through as a teenager

8

with divorced parents. His parents were never together, so he was shifted back and forth

between the two. R'Mell smiled and turned to look at Dre, realizing that the fire she felt, so long ago, still burned.

Even though Dre has always been there for her, R'Mell had suspicions about him. He was secretive. Very secretive. Dre would disappear for days without calling, then show up like she just saw him hours ago. She never thought he was cheating or running from someone. R'Mell's curiosity regarding Dre's behavior guided her to find out more about Dre. When Dre was on one of his disappearing acts, R'Mell went to the library. She noticed there were computers there. Sitting at table alongside students and seniors, R'Mell typed in Dre's name. Tears fell down her cheeks as she read article after article. One specific article tore her world apart. The headline read "L.A.'s Triple Threat". Pictured were Miguel Garcia, Rich Reeves, and her father. Details she never expected. Although heartbroken and in shock, R'Mell never repeated what she discovered, which has probably kept her alive all these years.

Memories of good times rush through her sleepy head as they drove out of the city for the very last time. However, they had bad times too. Too many. The drug game was deadly and unpredictable. No one got out of the game and lived to tell the story. Especially not who they were dealing with. All anyone can do is try to run from the game. And that's exactly what they are doing. Running. Neither of them is weak at all. R'Mell and Dre don't want anything else to happen to the rest of their families. To keep them safe, they know this is what needs to be done.

Chicago did them wrong. Between the streets and job losses, they couldn't keep a cover life. When selling' drugs gives up a ghetto fabulous lifestyle, you gotta have a cover life to explain how you got what you got. If it weren't for "The Man", Miguel Garcia, they would have had a simple life. Miguel Garcia supplied all of Chicago and had thousands of people working for him. He is an evil and ruthless man who will kill anyone who messes with his money. People hate him, but not his money. As for R'Mell and Dre, everything went south when they decided to move on. The money started coming slowly, and people around them kept dying. All they wanted was out, and this was the best way to do it. There was no rest for the weary, and they were just tired.

Dre stands 6'4" tall with a medium build. He has sleepy brown eyes, shoulder-length dreads, and a sexy goatee. But it was his smile that melted R'Mell's heart over 20 years ago. Dre has always been her better half. He loves her in and out, but will check her when she's wrong. Dre has two sisters: he's the baby. Between his mother and his sisters, he knows "the two sides of every woman". As he sees it, there is a feminine side that is nurturing and sensitive. Then there is the "man side," which is the evil and petty side. "How you treat a woman is the side you get", says Dre. R'Mell has shown him both of her "sides," and he still loves her. The life they've led has brought out the "man side" of her more over the years, and Dre realized they are better together than apart. He never met a woman who could hold her own and not fall to pieces when business needed to be done. He understands her. He understands why she does the things she does. He knows her heart. He never questions her thinking or doubts her methods. Dre will follow R'Mell anywhere and through anything. Dre deeply loves R'Mell. Although he makes the moves, she is the mastermind—and only they know it.

R'Mell had no adult role model in her life to guide her. Her parents separated when she was a little girl, so she learned everything in life by trial and error. She was a very lonely child despite having an older sister and a younger brother. R'Mell learned early how to disappear in a room without leaving it. When their parents separated, they all grew up in different ways. For R'Mell, she was abused every way you could think of and held all that childhood trauma inside. With no caring family or friends, she had no outlet to talk to anyone about it. She lost trust in people before she was 15. As a teen, she realized from watching TV and reading books that what she endured was abuse. No child should have had to go through what she did.

She felt too embarrassed and scared to tell anyone until she met Dre. After a few months together, she finally told him. Until then, R'Mell believed her life was normal. Her life was just like that of any other girl. Dre explained to her that it wasn't and helped her suppress the hate she developed toward her family for letting it happen for so long. R'Mell believed all men were like her abuser except Dre. He showed her love and compassion. He helped her see how beautiful she really is. R'Mell stands 5'9" tall with feminine curves and long brown hair that sits in the middle of her back. Dre showed her how she compared to all the models in Jet magazine. His love for her helped her temporarily forget her childhood and focus on being with him. Although she was angry and confused, R'Mell knew then that she was no longer alone in the world. She owes Dre, and she will protect what they have at any cost. Dre wouldn't do anything reckless if it put her in danger. He just wouldn't.

"R'Mell! Wake up!" shouted Dre, shaking her up from a dead sleep.

"What's wrong?" shouted R'Mell, sitting up from a lounging position in the passenger seat.

"We got company! A black old school has been tailing us since I pulled onto the freeway", Dre said nervously. "Grab the burner!" R'Mell reached under her seat, pulled out the 9mm, and placed it in her lap. She glanced in the side-view mirror and saw the car creeping up on her side, two cars back.

The roaring of the car's engine sounded as if a lion were chasing them. Without hesitation, she pointed the gun out the window. *Bang! Bang! Bang!* One shot hit the old school car's front windshield as Dre switched lanes. The old school pulled back and veered off to the side of the road. Dre floored it, pushing 100 miles an hour to get away.

R'Mell put the gun back under her seat and kept a lookout for the old school car. *This ride looks like the one parked across the street all week,* she thought. She never mentioned it to Dre. It could just be a coincidence or a different car. R'Mell didn't see it anymore, so she told Dre to slow down.

"Slow down, babe. I don't want to do this shit anymore! I don't want to live like this anymore. This shit is crazy!" cried R'Mell as her hand shook with the metallic taste of fear in her mouth.

"I know, babe. We almost free. Once we get to Los Angeles and start our new jobs, we will be alright. Our lives will change for the better, and we won't have to look over our shoulders all the damn time. Just wait and see. We gone be straight" said Dre.

A couple of hours later, Dre pulled into a motel off the freeway to catch their breath and get some rest. They have been through hell in the past few hours and need a chance to collect their thoughts and plan. After checking into the motel, they each took a four-hour shift to sleep, with R'Mell taking first watch. She was still on edge and couldn't relax. While Dre snored, R'Mell started thinking of her own plan. She had to keep it real with herself about everything she'd been through with Dre. She has changed for love, now look where it has gotten her. There were more good times than bad, she admitted to herself, but the bad times far outweighed the good. Dre has been the love of her life, but the cost of love is sometimes deadly.

As she sits in the dark, peeping behind the curtains, she sees a sheriff's car approach the motel. The car pulls into the parking lot and parks. The officer just sits there with the engine idle. Suddenly, a female exits the room next door and gets in the sheriff's car. The sheriff puts the car in reverse and slowly drives over to where the dumpsters are at the end of the building. R'Mell walks around the table inside her room to get a better look from the opposite side of the window. She can't see the entire car, but she notices it moving up and down. R'Mell laughs to herself. About 10 minutes later, she hears a car door slam shut and sees the female from next door walking back toward her room, lighting a cigarette. The sheriff drives out of the parking lot fast, but not without R'Mell catching the car number.

The sun glowed through the curtains, directly into Dre's eyes, when R'Mell changed seats for the third time. In the past five hours, she had seen the sheriff get some, two drug deals, a hoe get her ass beat for trying to steal a trick's wallet while he slept, and the manager get a blowjob behind the same dumpster. With all the drama going on outside, R'Mell didn't have time to get sleepy.

"Why you let me sleep so long, babe?' asked Dre in his morning raspy voice while rolling over in bed.

"I have been entertained this whole time with the drama goin' on outdoors that I didn't realize it. You good to drive?" laughed R'Mell as she kissed Dre on the forehead.

Dre rose off the bed to put on his clothes, then headed to the bathroom. "Yeah, I'm good," he said while stretching against his morning flow that R'Mell hated to hear every morning.

"You ready to get outta here, Mell?" asked Dre while yawning and flushing the toilet.

Walking into the bathroom with Dre, she replied, "Yeah, just need to wash up first." As they both washed their hands, a knock was at the door. R'Mell and Dre both froze, looking surprised.

"I'll get it", said R'Mell.

R'Mell opened the room door to see the office manager standing there. "May I help you?" asked R'Mell with a look of frustration.

"Good morning. I just wanted to let you folks know that there's a home-cooked breakfast ready in the office. Please come help yourselves." Said the office manager with a smile, with dirty teeth and stringy hair.

"Thank you, we will be right down to check out," R'Mell said with a returned smile and closed the door.

"Since when do motels offer home-cooked breakfast? I need to get out more, I guess. Or maybe, he made breakfast cause he got a blowjob behind the dumpster a couple hours ago. Either way, he don't look like he clean cause he got on the same clothes from when we checked in last night", rambled R'Mell.

Dre stares at R'Mell, laughing and asks, "What the hell are you talkin' about, Mell? Let's get somethin' else to eat and get on down the e-way."

With 2,000 miles of memories and stress behind them, three days later, R'Mell and Dre finally arrived in sunny Los Angeles. The weather was much different from that in Chicago. It was mid-March, and Chicago still had snow on the ground when they left. R'Mell closed her eyes and took the sun into her face while admiring the tall palm trees that seemed to be everywhere. They immediately go to R'Mell's cousin Dee's house on Hoover Street in South Los Angeles. R'Mell envies Dee because she seems to have it all. The house, the car, and four kids. She got out of the game five years ago from prostitution and dancin'. She ran from her pimp and never looked back. R'Mell secretly wanted Dee's life, but she will have her own new life soon. She and Dre must first find a house.

They both have jobs that start on Monday. Dee's house was in the middle of the block. A long, terra-cotta colored one-story. Thugs hanging out front. Kids riding bikes in the driveway.

Ring! Ring! R'Mell rings Dee's doorbell, then hears footsteps running to the door. A little, pretty-faced girl opens the door.

"Who are you?" she asked, with big brown eyes and two ponytails.

"I'm your cousin R'Mell. Is your mommy home?" asked R'Mell. The little girl looked R'Mell up and down before she yelled, "Mom, there's some lady at the door for you, sayin' she's my cousin! Should I let her in?"

Dee peeked around the door and said, "Girl, go sit down! Hey, cuz, when did you get in? Come on in. Where's Dre?" hugging R'Mell.

"Oh, he's at the car getting the bags. How are you?" asked R'Mell with a smile.

Dee is R'Mell's first cousin on her father's side. She and R'Mell favor each other in the face, but Dee is thinner than R'Mell due to her being a breast cancer survivor. Breast cancer also runs in her mother's side of the family. R'Mell and Dee have kept in touch with each other since they were teenagers. They would do anything for each other.

"Well, I don't mean to be rude, cuz, but Gabriella's friends have taken my guest room over for a sleepover tonight. I'm sorry, but I have no more room for you and Dre to stay with us tonight. I didn't know you were coming. Why didn't you call me first, cuz?" asked Dee with aggression in her tone.

"It was a last-minute decision. I should have called on the road. It's alright. We can find a hotel somewhere," replied R'Mell.

Dre comes walking up the driveway behind R'Mell, out of breath with all their luggage, and says, "Hey, Dee. How ya been, cuz?"

"Good", replied Dee, rolling her eyes.

"Sorry, babe, but we have to find a hotel for the night. Dee has company over", states R'Mell in a sarcastic voice.

Dre looks at R'Mell, with irritation on his face, then at Dee, and says, "Ok, see ya later, Dee" as he turns and walks away.

"Okay, cuz, we're gonna go. Talk with you soon," says R'Mell as she hugs her goodbye.

R'Mell walks down the driveway and gets into the car, then turns and asks Dre, "What do you think?"

"About what?" answers Dre in a tired, sarcastic tone.

"You don't think anybody's got to her, do you?" asks R'Mell.

Dre's phone buzzes, and he flips it over. R'Mell

looked at Dre, puzzled. *Why wouldn't he answer his phone?* She pushed the negative thought away before it could finish forming.

"No. Now let's find a hotel and get some sleep. I'm exhausted from all this driving", yawned Dre, putting the truck in drive and driving off. R'Mell wasn't convinced. As she stared out the window, she felt guilty for thinking Dee would betray her, but she just felt uncomfortable. People had betrayed her before. Dre wasn't people, but maybe she, too, was just tired and needed some rest. They drove on Imperial Highway until they found a hotel with a vacancy. As soon as they checked in and dropped their bags in the corner of the room, they both took showers and laid down exhausted. "Mell, half my body wants to blow yo back out right now. But the other half is numb," laughed Dre.

Laughing, R'Mell replied, "All I can do is lie here like a fuckin' log, anyway. I'm tired as a bitch!"

Turning onto their sides to face each other, they kissed and recited their good night, "I love you," then turned back-to-back. With both of their backs touching each other, R'Mell was still bothered by Dee's reaction to them showing up at her house. Was it because she really did have a sleepover for her daughter, or was it because someone from Chicago already got to her? She would have to talk to Dee again and let her know that they left that life and want to live as she does. No games, just livin' a normal life that everyone dreams about. Dre lay quietly, trying to figure out his next move and how to tell R'Mell the truth about his past. He has been putting the conversation off for months, and now that their lives have transformed into their current situation, he has no choice. He's back home. The city that groomed him. The city that took everything that meant anything to him. Dre is afraid the truth will break R'Mell's heart, but he has to tell her. There is no way he can continue to roam the city without being seen or people coming up to him. Before he makes any move, he has to look R'Mell in the eyes and let her know who he really is.

Ring! Ring! The hotel room phone rang the next morning, waking Dre. Dre reached for the phone and said, "Hello", in a raspy voice.

"Hello, sir. Check-out time was 11:00. Are you staying another day? If not, I need you out of the room in 10 minutes so it can be cleaned", stated the front desk clerk.

"Yeah, we'll be staying da' week. I'll be down in a minute to pay for it", said Dre and hung up the phone.

Dre reached over, attempting to wake R'Mell, but she was not in bed.

"Mell? You in the bathroom?" shouted Dre. No answer. In a panic, Dre got out of bed quickly and started to put his clothes on. Knock! Knock! Dre swung open the door fast, and there stood R'Mell with coffee, doughnuts, and a big smile.

"Morning baby. I left while you were sleeping 'cause I was hungry, but the only thing around here is a doughnut shop. I left without takin' the room key. Sorry if I woke you," rambled R'Mell.

Dre kissed R'Mell on the forehead while still dressing himself and said, "Good morning, Mell. Naw, you didn't wake me. The hotel staff did. I gotta go down to the front desk and pay for our room for the week. Give me the credit card, and I'll go find us some real food too."

As Dre was talking, R'Mell pulled apart the hotel-stripped curtains and let the world in. The sun was shining, and she could smell the donuts from the shop she had just left. She was in a good mood today, which was rare. Maybe this was the right move for them to make.

Dre grabbed the card from her hand and kissed R'Mell on the forehead. As Dre was leaving, R'Mell said, "I got a lead on a house from a lady at the doughnut shop. She said it's a gated community up in the hills. I thought that would be perfect for a while. I have her number. Her name is Bonita. Are you interested in seeing it today, babe?" asked R'Mell.

"Yeah, we can go look at it. I'll be back soon. Love you," said Dre while closing the hotel room door.

R'Mell knew what Dre was on. He was gonna get with his L.A. connect and get some money flowin' in. He has a couple of people out in Lancaster that he dealt with when they were in Chicago. Now that they are in L.A., prices for work would be lower. Even though moving to L.A. happened unexpectedly, she knows Dre will keep them safe until she gets a feel of her new surroundings.

That afternoon, Dre returned to the room with a bunch of fast food and a pocket full of money. Now that he was back in L.A., it was business as usual. He checked in with his P.O. to check in, but also began the paperwork to transfer probation from Chicago. Then, a visit to his lawyer to let him know he was back for good. Finally, he met with his crew and filled them in on his current situation and game plan. He stopped by his place, got some money from the safe, and headed back to the hotel.

"Where did you get that from?" R'Mell asked, regretting the question as soon as she asked. *He's starting to*...she began to think, but stopped.

"Don't ask, don't tell. Remember?", Dre said.

"I know", R'Mell said softly. Then she hopped up happily, kissed Dre on the lips, and said, "What you get me? I'm starvin' like Marvin."

They ate Tam's while sitting on the king-sized bed, watching Maury uncover another mother lying about how she's 100% sure he's the daddy.

Dre took a deep breath, muted the TV, then looked at R'Mell.

"Babe, why you mute the TV? We was watchin' that," asked

R'Mell with a mouth full of fries.

"We need to talk," responded Dre with nervousness in his voice. Noticing the look in his eyes and the sound of his voice, R'Mell paused with a look of concern on her face.

Grabbing Dres's hand, R'Mell asked, "Baby, what's up?"

Just then, some kids were playing loudly, running outside their window. They both suddenly turned toward the window to see a man and woman carrying bags and smaller children in their arms slowly behind them.

Returning to each other, staring face to face, Dre began speaking.

"Mell, what I have to tell you is gonna start some shit between us and this city. Remember the night we met..." R'Mell thinks of that day in her head daily. She looks at Dre, thinking, *Is this the day he's finally gonna come clean?* She's been waiting for this day for seven years, and now that they are in Los Angeles, Dre must reveal his truth.

R'Mell replies, "Of course, I do. What's this about, Dre?"

Raising his finger to her lips, Dre continued, "Let me finish. The night I met you was the night before I landed in Chicago. I ain't grow up there, as I told you. I just met my dad's fam the night before. My cousins wanted to take me out to the spot they hustled at to get my feet wet. So, when I met you, things changed for me. I never wanted to be in the streets, like my father. But my father sent me to Chicago. He wanted me to get a feel of the life and learn how he did. See, he was the main connect in Chicago when I was born. He broke bread wit the family he sent me to, as a protégé. I was introduced to who I needed to be introduced to and flown to Mexico when it was time to re-up..."

R'Mell sat quietly, but her blood was boiling on the inside because she now realizes everything that has happened in the past seven years has been about him and his father. The friends and family they lost. All the robberies, the shootouts; all because of him. She started staring into space, thinking of how to react to his confession. Once she realized she would also tell her truth, she turned to Dre, continuing his.

"So, when you didn't hear from me, I was handlin family business, back here wit my father. I was still in school; that was my cover. My father made sure I had sumthin to fall back on in case he felt I couldn't cut it", paused Dre as he stood up and started pacing the floor. Seeing that R'Mell had no expression on her face, he assumed she was still listening and continued.

"Fast forward to a year and a half ago, when I said we needed our own spot, my father sent me back to take over the South Side. I ain't wanna bring you in' cause I ain't want this for you. I want my own family with kids, a house, and a dog. Well, you know the rest of the story. But the most important part is that, ever since my father's death..."

Dre sat back down in front of R'Mell, took her hand in his, and continued to say, "I been runnin' south Chicago and Los Angeles. I'm more of a boss here than I was there..."

Looking deep into R'Mell's eyes and gently stroking the side of her face, Dre said, "Stepping into my father's shoes here means I can give you everything and anything you ever told me you wanted..."

Looking back in Dres's eyes, R'Mell returned a fake smile with her head cocked to the side and said, "Are you through?"

Dre jerked his hand down in confusion and shouted, "What the fuck you mean, am I through? I just tried to explain to you some real shit that I been keepin from you this whole time, and yo fucked up response is are you through?" Dre rose from the bed, pissed off, and grabbed his wallet and keys, heading for the door when R'Mell stated, "Now let me tell you sumthin."

Dre paused, looked over at R'Mell, heated, and threw his wallet and keys on the dresser and replied, "Tell me what, Mell?"

R'Mell said," I listened to you, now you listen to me. Come sit back down."

Dre walked back over to the bed and sat down. His face turned from being pissed off to looking scared because he knows R'Mell is going to say she going back to Chicago.

R'Mell held Dres's hand and said, "I've been waiting seven years to hear you tell me the truth. But the truth is, I already knew. After the night we met, I did a background check on yo ass. I knew who you were, where you came from, and who Rich Reeves was..."

Now Dre was even more confused, but relieved. He really felt she was gonna leave him once she knew the truth. He breathed a sigh of relief and continued to listen as R'Mell slid off the bed and began to pace the floor.

"My father didn't raise no fool. He raised an independent, strong, and smart-ass version of himself. He taught me the game when I was 12. Did it ever occur to you how I knew what to do when shit hit the fan? Did it ever occur to you how you were able to come up on the South Side wit no blowback? Did it EVER occur to you how you and yo uncle were able to get to and from Mexico wit no problem? Dre, I found out our fathers grew in the game under Miguel Garcia! And because I believe in loyalty to my father, I never told you I knew who you were. I never met your father, but I know our fathers were close..."

Dre stood up, scratching his head, and asked, "So you tellin' me all this time you knew who I was but said nothin'?" Dres' head was blown clean off his shoulders by the words R'Mell just assaulted him with.

Suddenly, gunshots broke through the window, and R'Mell and Dre dropped to the floor. They looked at each other and realized the burners were in the truck; they were defenseless. Shots continued to come through the room for over two minutes. R'Mell and Dre covered each other from the debris and glass that was flying through the room. Someone in a red hoodie flew past their window, running fast. Then the shots stopped, and they heard car tires screech away. Dre slowly lifted himself off the floor and looked out the window to see a man lying on the ground, dead, next to a car in the parking lot.

"You good?" shouted Dre to R'Mell.

"Yeah, I'm ok! What the fuck! I'm tired of getting' shot at and I ain't did shit to nobody! And now, I can't even eat my damn food!" yelled R'Mell as she got up from the floor to join Dre, peeking out the window.

"Babe, be quiet. I'm trying to hear what's going on", whispers Dre.

Attempting to hear what's going on outside, Dre hears the voice of the front desk clerk and a woman screaming. "Call 9-1-1, call 9-1-1!"

R'Mell goes over to the window to see what's going on. A man was lying stretched out on the ground in a pool of blood. She turned to Dre and asked, "What should we do?"

"We ain't finna do shit! That shit ain't got nothin' to do wit' us!", shouted Dre.

"Do we really want to be here when the cops come to question everybody? Shit, I know I don't", stated R'Mell nervously.

Dre turned to R'Mell and said, "We ain't do nothin wrong. We just as much victims as that muthafucka down there on the ground. So just chill, alright?"

"And you need to control that mouth of yours. It's gonna get us in trouble one day", Dre said to R'Mell, in a stern voice.

Looking at R'Mell's face with her arms crossed, Dre said somberly, "Ok, come on. Let's get outta here before the cops come."

Rushing to gather their things, they heard the police sirens. "Hurry up!" shouted Dre.

"I'm tryin'!" shouted R'Mell as she was throwing their stuff in anything to get outta there.

Before they could finish, there was the sound of a bullhorn yelling, "Everyone in the hotel, please come out with your hands up!"

Dre and R'Mell stopped what they were doing and stared at each other.

"Oh shit! What are we gonna do? We can't talk to the police," whispered R'Mell.

"Calm down. They just want to make sure the shooters ain't hidin' in the hotel. All they gone do is come look in the room and see that we were shot at and we not the shooters. There are bullet holes everywhere. The burner is in the car, on the street, not on the premises. We don't have any burners in the room. We good. Just follow my lead," said Dre. Dre noticed R'Mell's tension. As they both stared into each other's eyes, their hands locked together as they leaned in toward each other headfirst. Dre kissed R'Mell's forehead and whispered, "It's gonna be okay, my beautiful black butterfly. It's gone be okay". R'Mell shook her head up and down to let him know she is calm now. Safe.

They both went outside and stood by the door to their room with their hands up. Police officers and SWAT were everywhere. All R'Mell and Dre could do was stand still and look at what was going on. Officers were going through every room searching for anything that could help them figure out who killed the man on the ground and why. Down in the parking lot, an officer put a yellow plastic sheet over the man's body and taped off the scene. R'Mell looked on with a blank stare, remembering all the dead bodies she had seen back in Chicago.

They both turned simultaneously to notice a detective and three officers walking toward them.

"Hello, folks. You may put your hands down. I'm Detective Simmons, and I will be the lead detective on this case. I will be the one you call if you have any questions or recall any information. Now, how long have you been staying at the hotel?" he asked.

"We just checked in last night. We just moved here from Chicago", returned Dre with a calm voice.

"Are either of you hurt? I see a lot of bullet holes in your walls. We have the Salvation Army on the way to help you folks with shelter for the night. Can I see your identification, please?", asked Detective Simmons

R'Mell didn't say a word. She was too nervous to even open her mouth. There was nothing for her to say anyway. Dre told her to follow him. If Dre gives up his identification, then she will too. Until then, she will just shut up and be still. Police love to pull out a gun on you if you move too quickly.

"Yeah, we good. We don't need the Salvation Army. We'll find another hotel", said Dre as he pulled his wallet from his back pocket.

Dre nudged R'Mell to give him her ID. She wondered what Dre was doing. R'Mell reached into her hoodie, got out her ID, and handed it to the detective. Dre handed over his, too.

"Thank you, kindly. I'll be right back", stated Detective Simmons as he walked down the stairs to his squad car.

When the detective walked away with their IDs, R'Mell turned to Dre and asked, "Why did we give him our shit?"

"Neither of us has any warrants or been to jail in California, so we straight. He checking to see if we wanted. He'll be right back. Watch" said Dre.

Dre was a little nervous. He was hoping that the detective wasn't doing a nationwide search. He just left his lawyer's office earlier, so the transfer couldn't have happened that fast.

"Stand on ten. Here he comes", whispered Dre.

R'Mell was nervous as hell. Looking at the detective coming towards them, he looked to be moving in slow motion. *Bougie bitch, activate*, she said to herself with a smile on her face to hide her nervousness. R'Mell hasn't been in L.A. since a teenager, so she doesn't have anything to worry about. She's more worried about Dres' name.

"Just a couple of questions. Did either of you know the deceased?" asked Detective Simmons.

"Man, like I said, we just moved here. We don't know anybody here", replied Dre.

"Did you see anything? The deceased arguing with anyone? A car? Anything?" asked Detective Simmons.

"Naw. We were on the floor once we heard the shots. We didn't get up or move until we heard the officer on that loud ass bullhorn. Neither of us got hit or anything. We alright, thanks, detective", said Dre.

"Ok, folks, you are free to go. Unfortunately, I'm gonna have to ask you not to leave California for a few days until I can get your statements on record and control of this case", said Simmons as he handed back their IDs.

"Aight", said Dre. Dre recognized the detective, but the detective didn't recognize him. This was one of his father's pawns when he was alive. Detective Simmons was in his father's pocket but kept him five steps ahead of the LAPD when shit was hitting too close to home. Nonetheless, he knows Dre was by his name; they used to be childhood friends.

R'Mell and Dre turned to walk back into their room when Detective Simmons shouted, "Oh yeah, welcome to Los Angeles!"

R'Mell and Dre looked at each other like "this muthafucka crazy". Seeing as though they were out of the clear, they left the hotel room and got into their truck. The parking lot was chaotic. Pulling out of the parking lot slowly, it seemed as if all the officers were staring at them. Knowing they would cross paths with Detective Simmons again.

Dre had to be honest with himself. He was shook. There was too much janky shit happening on this trip. Between the old school cars following them to their hotel room, getting shot up. Dre was wondering if he and R'Mell should have left

Chicago. It seems they are being followed and stalked. No matter what, he has to keep them safe. But how? He knows who is behind all of this, but can't be sure.

"Let's go see Diamond and Chance. I haven't let them know we are in town yet and we need a place to crash until we find something of our own", stated Dre. Dre didn't want to take R'Mell to his house until it was set up. He needed a couple more days for his crew to finish everything he requested.

"Ok. I still have that information, Ms. Bonita, that I met at the doughnut shop gave me. The rent is reasonable for L.A. and not too far from Diamond and Chance off of LaBrea. I can't wait to see Diamond and the kids", replied R'Mell. On a cross street like Crenshaw & Slauson, the neighborhood hums with that familiar L.A. tension, not dangerous, just alive. Cars roll through with sun-faded paint jobs and rattling speakers. A Metro bus sighs as it pulls to the curb, releasing a wave of heat and impatience. Corner stores buzz with people grabbing cold drinks, and the murals, chipped but proud, watch over everything like guardians of the block. R'Mell smiled with excitement for their fresh start.

Thirty minutes later, approaching the driveway of Diamond and Chance's house, they could see the kids outside playing in the front yard. Chance was on the barbecue grill. The weather was a typical Los Angeles sunny day. No breeze, just humidity. As they drove to the front of the house, Chance noticed the car and smiled. "Diamond, they're here!" shouted Chance. He wiped his hands on a towel and raced over to the car.

Chance is the kind of man who carries silence like a weapon and presence like a warning. Tall, dark, and fine as hell, he moves with quiet confidence that makes people step aside without knowing why. His skin is chocolate colored and smooth, his features carved with a precision that feels almost unfair, and his eyes are deep, steady, and unreadable; they hold stories he'll never tell.

He's built like someone who's had to protect himself and others his whole life. Broad shoulders, big hands, and a walk that says he's always aware of every exit, every angle, every intention in the room. But beneath that hard exterior is a man defined by loyalty. Chance doesn't give his trust easily, but once he does, it's unbreakable. His best friend? Protected without question. His family? Sacred. His word? Ironclad. He's the one who shows up when things get messy, the one who handles what others can't, the one who keeps the people he loves safe, even if it means stepping into the shadows to do it.

A man with a past he doesn't speak on, a code he never breaks, and a heart he guards like a vault. Chance is the storm and the shelter, the kind of man who can be both the danger and the protection, depending on who you are to him.

"Hey, you guys made it! How was the drive?", giving Dre a manly hug as he got out of the car.

"We alive, bro. I'll tell you about it later. Where's my sister?" asked Dre.

Opening the front door and shouting, "Hey y'all, come on in!", Diamond waved them in.

Diamond is the kind of woman whose presence doesn't just enter a room, it claims it. Her skin glows like warm bronze under soft light, her features sculpted with a quiet elegance, and her eyes are brown, deep, almond-shaped, and expressive.

They carry a softness that can flip to darkness at the blink of an eye. She's a woman who knows exactly who she is and refuses to shrink for anyone. Her voice is smooth, warm, and steady, the kind that can calm storms or call someone out with a single sentence.

Diamond is as loyal as they come. The kind of wife who stands beside her man, not behind him. She understands Chance in ways no one else does; the shadows he carries, the weight he shoulders, the silence he hides behind. And she loves him not in spite of it, but through it. She's his balance, his anchor, his clarity when the world gets loud. But Diamond is not defined by Chance. She's her own force. Sharp-minded, intuitive, and emotionally intelligent. She reads people quickly, moves strategically, and carries a quiet power that makes others underestimate her until it's too late. Her strength isn't aggressive; it's intentional. Controlled. Elegant. The kind of strength that doesn't need to announce itself.

"Here, bro. Let me help you with your bags. You stayin' wit us right? We won't take no for an answer," stated Chance.

"Uncle Dre!" shouted the little boy carrying a football. Darren is five years old and loves to play football. He carries his ball around with him wherever he goes. Dre bought it for him. Running up to Dre, Darren jumped in his arms and gave Dre a big hug. As Darren got down, Dre asked, "Where's your sister?"

"She's in the tree house, playing with her dolls. I'll go get her", said Darren as he ran around the house.

"Got scotch? I'm ready for a drink!" said Dre to Chance.

"I got chu' bro", said Chance.

Waiting patiently for the men to finish, R'Mell cleared her throat and said, "Hello, Chance. It's nice to finally meet you in person", kissing him on the cheek as she walked into the house behind Dre.

They all walked into the house to see Diamond sitting in the living room. She had on a long-striped dress with her hair in a bun. There was an aura about her that R'Mell could see that was sad. But R'Mell kept it to herself. R'Mell has known Diamond since day one. They became as close as sisters can be, but today is their first time being in each other's physical presence. Phone and video calls have sustained them over the years, but she's excited to finally be able to hug and kiss them all.

"Dre, Mell!" shouted Diamond as she gave them both a hug and kiss. "Please sit down, take a load off. So how was your trip?" she asked.

"Chance, that drink," stated Dre.

"You ladies get caught up. Us gentlemen are gonna be in the study", said Chance.

Dre kissed R'Mell and Diamond, then followed Chance.

"Girl, what's up wit' Dre? Is he o.k.?" asked Diamond.

"Yeah, he's o.k. Just a long trip, you know. So, what's up with you? I love the house. Give me a tour," said R'Mell, redirecting the conversation.

"Sure, sis. Come on.", stated Diamond.

Diamond led R'Mell into the kitchen first. As she started to close the kitchen curtains, she noticed a black old-school car sitting on the edge of their driveway. She went to the back door and called the kids inside. R'Mell was admiring their breakfast nook as Diamond got a gun from the pantry. Diamond opened the curtains with the barrel of the gun to see that the car was now gone. She then ran into the study and shouted to Chance, "That car's back!"

Chance and Dre ran to the kitchen door, but the car was gone. They both ran outside to the edge of the driveway, looking down at both ends of the street.

Dre said to Chance, "Bro, what car? What the fuck is goin' on?"

"Come on back inside, bro. I'll tell you later", replied Chance as he guided Dre back inside and locked the door.

The house was beautiful. Tall ceilings with colorful sheer curtains throughout. Each room had a different color scheme. Even the bathrooms were colorful. The kids' rooms were sports and ballerina-themed. The master bedroom was as big as a studio apartment but elegantly furnished. R'Mell hoped to have a house like this with kids someday soon herself.

Back in the living room, R'Mell whispered to Diamond as she sat next to her on the couch, "Sis, what the hell is going on? What did you see out there?"

"Sis, no disrespect, if Chance did not speak on it, I won't either," replied Diamond. All R'Mell could do was shake her head to agree and change the subject until the men came to them to discuss it. *At least for now,* she thought.

"You have a beautiful house, Diamond. How do you manage it all with working and the kids?" asked R'Mell.

Shaking her head, Diamond says, "Girl, I pray. It's not easy. With Chance being on the road so much and work, I barely have any me time. The kids drain every ounce of energy I have. And my job is stressful enough."

"Speaking of jobs, Dre and I have interviews tomorrow," said R'Mell, redirecting the conversation again.

"Oh, really? Where?" asked Diamond.

"Dre has an interview with Smith & Company, a construction company, and I will be interviewing with REMAX. We both need these jobs. We need our own place. I appreciate you putting us up tonight, Diamond. We really had nowhere else to go", said R'Mell.

Diamond knows that's not true, but it's not her place to say anything. Her loyalty is to her brother and Chance. Until Dre speaks on his life in L.A., she will keep R'Mell clueless for her safety.

"Now you know you and my brother can stay here as long as you need to. We love you both", stated Diamond.

"Just then, Dayja came running into the living room where they both were seated. "Auntie Mell!" Dayja is Darren's identical twin and usually very quiet, but today she is loud and full of energy. Dayja hugged R'Mell, then asked for her Uncle Dre. "Your uncle is in the study with your dad right now, sweetheart", said Diamond.

"Uh oh! What did Uncle Dre do?" Dayja asked Diamond.

Diamond laughed, "Uncle Dre is not in any trouble. They are just talking."

"Oh, o.k., mommy," stated Dayja as she ran up to her bedroom to play.

"Chance takes the children into his study when they have been bad. That's why she asked that, Mell," stated Diamond.

"I was wondering," laughed R'Mell.

Suddenly, the door to the study opened, and both women looked at their husbands' faces as they walked out to the backyard. They looked upset. Wondering what was wrong, Diamond asked, "What do you suppose that's about?"

"I don't know, but I'm going to find out," stated R'Mell, getting up from the couch.

"No, no. Let them be, Mell. Let's get you guys settled into the guest room," said Diamond, stopping R'Mell from following the guys outside.

R'Mell knew Dre must have filled Chance in on their trip. Chance will then fill in Diamond later. Knowing how Chance and Diamond are, they will be safe. R'Mell followed Diamond to the guest room and helped her prepare the room. Out of the bedroom window, she could see her husband and Chance talking. After dinner, she and Dre will have to continue the conversation they started at the hotel.

After having a barbecue and a few drinks, R'Mell was ready for bed. She had gotten a little tipsy but still needed to make sure Dre was o.k. The men were back in the study, while she and Diamond were in the living room in front of the fire. The kids were in bed. R'Mell knocked on the door of the study. They had interviews tomorrow, and it could be the start of their new lives here in L.A. Tomorrow is very important to them both, and she didn't want anything to go wrong.

"I'll be up in a few, Mell," shouted Dre through the door.

"Ok!" shouted back R'Mell.

R'Mell turned toward Diamond and said, "Once again, thank you for letting us stay here, Diamond. We really appreciate it. I'm gonna turn in and get us unpacked."

Diamond hugged R'Mell and replied, "Anything for family. Get a good night's sleep so you can get that job tomorrow. Love ya girl."

It was just turning 10 o'clock, and the moon was keeping R'Mell awake. Plus, Dre hadn't come up to bed yet. She wonders what Dre and Chance have been talking about all this time. A part of her feels like they've been talking "business" all night, but they are close, so maybe they were just catching up. Either way, she just hopes he comes to bed soon.

Around midnight, Dre crept into the room, stumbling over the suitcases, trying to be quiet. Drunk, he just plops on the bed, awakening R'Mell.

"Sorry, babe. Go back to sleep", whispered Dre.

"Are you drunk?" questioned R'Mell with a smile on her face.

Speaking slowly, Dre replied, "No. And lower your loud ass voice before you wake everyone up. I'm here now. Go back to sleep."

R'Mell rolled over, out of love for Dre, cause she really wanted to cuss his ass out for talking to her like that. Instead, she lay awake, thinking, until she heard Dre snoring.

The next day, R'Mell and Dre went to their prospective interviews. R'Mell's interview went well, but she got the old "we'll call you" after. She felt horrible because she really wanted to hear "can you start immediately". However, Dre will start his construction job next Monday. R'Mell was at least relieved to hear that Dre got his job. A little jealous, but relieved. Nonetheless, it's only Tuesday. Maybe she will get a call back later in the week.

R'Mell and Dre went to Pinky's to celebrate that night. The line was long, but the food was great. After eating, they decided to go have a drink at The Elephant Bar.

"I'm so proud of us taking the steps we took to get here. It was a fucked-up trip, but it's been worth it so far. You have a job, and I'm going to see that apartment I was telling you about tomorrow. Looks like we comin' up, baby", said R'Mell as they made a toast.

Turning around in his barstool, Dre replied, "Yeah, baby, we makin' moves. But we still need to be careful. We ain't out of the woods yet." R'Mell was enjoying herself until Dre mentioned that.

Suddenly, a man walked up to R'Mell and asked her if he could buy her a drink. Dre looked at the man and said, "Have you lost yo mind, nigga! Don't you see me sittin' right here, bro? That's my wife you talkin' to! Get the fuck outta here!"

The man put his hands up and walked away. He then walked over to another man sitting in a booth with two other men. The man sitting in the center of the large table raised his

glass, with a smile, as if to say hello. Dre knew then it was getting ready to be some bullshit, and they obviously didn't know who he was.

"Come on, let's go", Dre quietly said to R'Mell. Neither of them had a burner, so they were sitting ducks if something popped off.

The man who was sitting at the table then jumped up and followed R'Mell and Dre out the door. Dre turned around and said, "What the fuck do you want?"

"I just want to compliment your lovely wife and give you a piece of advice," the man said.

He continued while walking closer to R'Mell and Dre and said, "Stay out of my bar and away from Los Angeles. This city is no place for a handsome couple like yourselves."

Just then, Dre took R'Mell's arm, and they started walking toward their truck. Staring deep into the man's eyes, Dre couldn't get too heated because then the man's posse came out of the bar and stood beside the man. All Dre could do, without a burner, was get R'Mell out of the way. He'd be back to deal with this situation at a later date. Dre realized he had been away for a while this time. Knowing that, he begins to think of what he needs to do to let Los Angeles remember who the Reeves Family is.

Old Friends, New Family

Wednesday was rainy and cold. The children couldn't go out, so they spent the day playing video games. This gave the adults some free time to gather in the living room. The fireplace was lit, and everyone had a corner of their own to relax. Then the doorbell rang.

"Who could that be?" asked Diamond.

"Be calm. I'll get it", said Chance, walking toward the door. Everyone's eyes followed Chance to the door as he opened it.

"Jazz, Dayzee, Staci? What are you ladies doing here?" shouted Chance with a smile.

"Freezin' our asses off out here! Are you gonna let us in, Chance?" shouted Jazz.

Skeptically, Chance said, "Yeah, come on in. Wipe your feet and take off your shoes."

"Everyone, this is our friend Jay. He helps us out on things from time to time," said Jazz.

After the ladies and Jay took off their shoes, Diamond greeted them at the door.

"Hey, what's up?" asked Diamond.

"We heard Dre was in town and finally brought R'Mell. So, we here to see him and meet our new family member. What up, Dre?" shouted Staci.

"What up, fam!", Dre said while standing up to hug Staci and the ladies. Dre hadn't heard from Jazz and Staci in years.

"What up, cuz?" said R'Mell to Dayzee while hugging her.

"This is Staci and Jazz, Mell. They fam", said Dayzee to R'Mell.

"Hello, ladies. Nice to meet you," replied R'Mell.

"So, what's up, Jazz. What's goin' on? Y'all know not to come to my home unless I tell you, so why in the hell are you really here?" said Diamond, staring Jay up and down, then back to the ladies with disgust.

Chance left the room to check on the children.

"We got a sweet lick in the works and need some assistance in carryin' out. We done most of the legwork already. We need muscle. So, we came to see if we can make a deal", said Jazz.

"What's the deal?" said Dre.

Diamond walked away when Dre spoke.

R'Mell looked at Dre. He returned a "it's ok, look". Chance returned to join in on the conversation.

"The deal is we need a nigga taken care of for half the lick", stated Jazz.

"We'd do it ourselves, but we in deep enough as it is. The shit's legit. It's in Miami. The mark is an accountant who has been in our pockets for way too long, and we need him gone. An appointment is set up to meet him on Friday at midnight at his office. He's givin' 100k in cash for his life. But we want what's in his safe, which is over a million cash and bonds. There is also a deed to my house in there I want back! Dre, he knows the girls and me already. He may have some muscle with him since he knows his life is in danger now. Y'all can make half a mill off this lick. Are you in?" asked Jazz, directly looking at Dre.

Jazz knew to direct her words at the man who really could use the money. Chance looked at Dre, then at Diamond, who was furious. Dre was pondering the thought of helping them out. *The money sounds good, but who are we really dealing with?* Dre thought to himself.

"Give me some time to think about it. I know you're on a deadline wit this nigga, so give me 'til midnight. I'll have Diamond contact you", Dre stated while motioning to R'Mell to get up.

Dre gently grabbed R'Mell's arm and pulled her to the side.

"Ok. Midnight it is. Thanks for hearin' me out. We out!" stated Jazz.

"Hold up, Jazz. How long have you known this nigga?" asked Dre.

"A couple years, he solid. I had him checked out before I hired him. Don't worry, he's o.k.," whispered Jazz.

"Bye", said Staci and Dayzee.

Diamond followed them outside and closed the door. Jay and the ladies stood in front of her, knowing they were finna get cussed out.

"Have you bitches lost yo fuckin minds! Coming to my house, unannounced, with a petty ass lick my son could do! If my brother hadn't spoken, you all would be dead right now. He saved yo sorry ass lives. Now get the hell away from my house until I call you, hoes!", hollered Diamond.

Jay rolled his eyes at Diamond, and she saw him. Diamond grabbed the back of his head, shoved a knife in his Adam's apple, and whispered in his ear, "Little bitch ass nigga, I don't know what these hoes didn't tell you about me, but they should have informed you who I am. If yo eyes are important to you, I suggest you keep them looking forward the next time you ever think of disrespecting me again."

Diamond licked Jay's ear and pushed him into Jazz. "Jazz, if you ever come back here, where my children and husband sleep, I will kill you, yo kids, and yo parents. All of you. Now get the hell outta here!", stated Diamond as she wiped off her blade and placed it back in her thigh belt. Jay and the ladies nodded and ran to their car at the end of the driveway and sped off. Once they were out of sight, Diamond turned to fix her dress and hair in the reflection of the glass before entering the house with a smile.

Dre turned and looked R'Mell in the eyes and said, "If I do this, we could be set. A new car. That apartment you want..."

"Oh shit! I forgot I have to go see that today!" shouted R'Mell.

Placing her hand on Dres's left cheek, R'Mell whispered with a smile, "Do what you must. I trust you. I love you, Dre. I know you will do whatever you need to do to make sure we straight. It's us against the world, baby!

"Now, I'm gonna go get ready to go see this apartment. Diamond, you wanna ride?" asked R'Mell.

"Naw, girl, you go ahead. The kids are here, and it's time for their nap anyway. Be careful and see you when you get back", said Diamond.

Chance and Dre gathered in the study again. This time, it would be to make a decision that would change their lives forever.

"Bro, how well do you know these hoes? Are they on the up and up or what? It seems like too easy a lick. I'm gonna send you, but take two of your goons wit chu. And come right back," stated Dre.

"Yeah, these are a couple of Diamonds girls and Dayzee. You remember, Dayzee. She's an old friend of R'Mell's, somehow. I forgot how. I don't know how Dayzee got mixed up wit them, but if she's in on it, then the lick must be legit. Dayzee lives for this shit. I'll go handle this shit for us. Does this mean we back in business, bro?" asked Chance with a smile and his hand out to shake Dres's hand.

"Yes, sir! The wives won't contest it cause of the loot involved, but we'll tell them tonight", said Dre.

R'Mell pushed in the address to the apartment on her phone and started up the truck. Out of nowhere comes Dayzee.

"You know where you goin', cuz? I can ride wit chu?", stated Dayzee.

R'Mell rolled down the window and said, "Yeah, I googled it. But if you wanna ride, come on."

Dayzee and Jay walked around to the passenger side and got it.

"You mind if I light up?" asked Dayzee.

"Naw, roll that shit. After the week I've had, I need to get high. So, what's up wit this lick?" asked R'Mell.

"It's legit. Jazz and Staci just want their money from the nigga. He been schemin' off the top of them for years. Now they want it back, that's all. You think we should have done it, huh? No muscle?" asks Dayzee.

Jay was quietly sitting in the back seat.

"Well, duh. It's them hoes' deal. Why ask niggas to do what a bitch can do easier? All they had to do was let him think he was gone get some. They could have taken the money. My guess is there is something dangerous about this nigga. I hope Chance can handle himself", said R'Mell.

"It will be easy peasy. Especially wit anotha nigga goin to collect. He ain't gone make it hard. Maybe on himself but not on Chance," replied Dayzee.

They all laughed as they pulled into the apartment complex. The building was made of brick, and everyone had either a patio or a balcony. R'Mell was hoping for a balcony. The landscaping was immaculate, and there was an Olympic-sized swimming pool that she could see through the gate. There were children in the pool playing and swimming. Someday soon, she hoped Dre would be ready to start their own family. *Maybe the new place would mellow him out some, so he'd change his mind about kids,* she thought as she parked the truck.

Just as R'Mell put the truck in park, out of nowhere comes this man at her driver's side window,

"You must be Mrs. Reeves. I'm Beauty, nice to meet you. And who are your friends?" asked Beauty as he reached to shake R'Mell's hand.

"We are none of yo business. We just here to support my girl in finding a place. Handle yo business. We won't be in y'all's way," stated Dayzee.

Beauty looked at Dayzee like she was crazy. He was about six foot five and 300 pounds. He definitely was no beauty, but was charming, nonetheless. Beauty wore neon pink shorts with a too-small white tee.

"No problem. Follow me, and I will take you upstairs to your new home. First, we need to stop at my apartment to get the keys," said Beauty as he made his way up the stairs, switching harder than a two-dollar whore.

Beauty opened the door to his apartment, and nothing but weed smoke came out. There were people everywhere in his living room. Some were even on the floor, and everybody had a blunt in their mouth.

"Excuse the place. My maid doesn't come until Monday. Ha, ha. That was a joke. Wait here while I find the keys," laughed Beauty.

R'Mell, Dayzee, and Jay all looked around the doorway once the smoke cleared. Then they looked at each other. They all stepped in and looked around. Everyone just looked at them like they had never seen black people before. One woman said, "Hey, y'all want a blunt?"

Before Dayzee could say a word, Beauty came from the back and shouted, "I found them. Let's go!"

As they walked down the hall to the elevator, Jay whispered, "Did you see those bricks on the table?"

"Shit, did you see the money on the table. This nigga a mark. We should let the girls know about this nigga. This the lick they should be thinkin' about, or we could just handle him ourselves", whispered Dayzee.

"You two ain't handlin' shit, especially wit me around. We tryin' to get this apartment. Don't talk about robbin' this fool, and he probably can hear you," whispered R'Mell.

While riding the elevator to the third floor, Beauty said, "The apartment is a two-bedroom and goes for $1800 a month. There's a balcony and air conditioning. No pets, and we have washers and dryers on the first floor. Any questions, Mrs. Reeves?"

"Yes, is this a safe neighborhood?" asked R'Mell.

"It's pretty quiet. We have 72 units here, so there is an occasional arguing amongst lovers or a loud party..."

"Like in your apartment?" asked Jay.

Beauty rolled his eyes at Jay and continued, "As I was trying to say, we have a quiet complex otherwise. There is an intercom system, so no one can get in the building unless they are buzzed in. People like that extra sense of security. We also have cameras throughout the building, and they are monitored by the security guards at the gate. The gate is open during the day but closed and monitored at night. Here we are."

The elevator doors opened to a long, bright white hallway with dark green carpeting. There was accent lighting in front of each apartment on both sides and a window at the end of the corridor. Apartment 305 is where they stopped. The door is double-bolted, so Beauty was fidgeting with the keys.

"Thought you had the right keys," said Dayzee.

Beauty ignored her.

Beauty got the right key and opened the door. Inside was a beautiful, bright, lit apartment. From the entryway, the living room had a sunken floor with royal blue carpeting. Walking in, you could smell the flowers from the trees outside the balcony. The kitchen was a nice size, and the bedrooms were huge. There were vertical blinds on all the windows, and ceiling fans in every room.

"This apartment is only $1800. What's the catch, Beauty?" asked R'Mell.

Jay and Dayzee were in the kitchen, whispering. R'Mell had a bad feeling about those two, but she'd just let Dre know when she got back to Chance and Diamond's house.

Beauty laughed and replied, "Yes, Mrs. Reeves. It's $1800 with $1000 security deposit. There is also a $35 credit and background check for each of you and Mr. Reeves. When did you want to move in?"

"As soon as possible!" exclaimed R'Mell.

"Ok then. Let's go back downstairs and get the applications. I'd like to be the first to welcome you to your new home, Mrs. Reeves. It will be a joy to have you both here", said Beauty with a smile.

"Blah, blah, blah. Can we go now? I'm hungry", said Jay.

"Yeah, me too", chimed in Dayzee.

"Let's go then. I would love to get the application from you first, though. My husband is gonna love this apartment", said R'Mell as they walked out of the apartment.

Beauty locked the door to the apartment and turned to R'Mell and said, "We'd love to have you."

The elevator opened, and they all walked in. Jay and Dayzee had strange looks on their faces, like kids when they were up to something. R'Mell looked at them and felt uncomfortable. The ride to the first floor was quiet. All you heard was the chimes of the elevator passing each floor. There was just an eerie feeling like something was about to happen. R'Mell knew these two were about to do some shady shit, but she was trying to be cool cause they needed their own spot.

Exiting the elevator, Jay and Dayzee walked way behind Beauty and R'Mell. As soon as Beauty opened the door, he turned and asked, "Would you like to come and have a celebratory blunt with us while I find you an application?"

"Hell yeah!" said Dayzee and Jay simultaneously as they rushed past Beauty and R'Mell straight into the apartment.

After seeing Dayzee and Jay rush in with Cheshire Cat smiles on their faces now, R'Mell shrugged her shoulders and said, "Sure, why not. But then we have to go."

Beauty disappeared again to the back room while each of them was handed a blunt by a pretty woman in a red sundress. Dayzee pulled out her weed zippo lighter and lit each of their blunts. All seats were taken but two on the couch. Jay hopped down, then pulled Dayzee with him, leaving R'Mell standing. She noticed no one in the kitchen, so she made her way.

Beauty returned from the back room with the application and a black box and said, "Now that we are all acquainted, let's turn this party up a notch!" He pulls out a quart-sized baggie with white powder in it, pushes everything off the coffee table onto the floor, and continues to say, "Let the games begin!"

R'Mell placed her unfinished blunt in the ashtray and motioned to Dayzee that she was ready to go. Dayzee tried to ignore her by looking away toward Jay. They started whispering in each other's ears and then stood up together. Relieved,

R'Mell walked toward the coffee table and began talking to the top of Beauty's head since he was taking in a line of coke.

"Thank you for the tour and the application. However, we must be going now. We don't want them coming to look for us", shouted R'Mell over the loud music and video game being played.

Coming up for air, Beauty handed R'Mell the application and waved bye without saying a word.

All three of them ran out of the apartment, laughing. As R'Mell pushed the elevator button, a few people also left the party from Beauty's apartment.

The lady in the red sundress was one of them. "Not everyone is into that type of party, but Beauty and his nephews. We just like to hang out and chill. We all live in 437. Come chill wit us when you move in", she said.

"Hi. I'm R'Mell, and your name is?", while reaching to shake the lady in red hand.

"I'm Sophia. Nice to meet you, R'Mell.

Once they got in the truck, Dayzee shouted, "I left my zippo! I'm going back to get it!"

Dayzee was halfway up the ramp when Jay shouted, "You're not going back up there by yo'self, I'm comin' too! Keep the truck running, R'Mell. We'll be right back!"

"Y'all ain't back in five minutes, I'm gone!" shouted R'Mell out the window. Dayzee and Jay ran up the ramp to the front door of the apartment building, then disappeared. R'Mell knew they were on bullshit, but she really wasn't gonna leave them hanging.

Ten minutes went by, and all of a sudden, R'Mell heard gunshots coming from inside the building. R'Mell started the truck and drove up to the curb as Jay and Dayzee were running out.

"Let's go! Go!" shouted Dayzee as she was running to the truck.

"What the fuck did y'all do?" shouted R'Mell as she sped out of the parking lot.

"Hey y'all, I got hit!" cried Jay as he held his shirt filled with blood.

"Stop playin', bro! We just hit a lick! Drive, Mell, drive!" shouts Dayzee as she turns to see Jay passed out in the back seat.

"Shit! Mell, drive to the nearest hospital so we can drop this nigga off!" shouted Dayzee.

R'Mell felt as if all her hopes and dreams had suddenly come to an end. These two have gotten her back into the world she and Dre were running from. Now this shit. No matter where they go, they seem to be in the middle of some shit, either they got themselves into, or someone else did. She found herself rocking back and forth, something she does when she's anxious. *Dre is gonna be so mad at me*, she thought. Driving 60 miles an hour to the nearest hospital was not in her plans today. Right or wrong, Beauty didn't deserve whatever Dayzee and Jay did.

"Quit daydreamin' and drive this damn truck!" shouted Dayzee.

"First of all, who the fuck are you hollerin' at, bitch! I'm going as fast as I can, whereas the cops won't stop us, Day! You and this nigga done fucked up my plans! Now you got me as an accessory to whatever the fuck y'all just did! Fuck you and that nigga! And yo bitch ass better not be bleeding on my seat, nigga!", shouted R'Mell.

Instantly, R'Mell's head started pounding and felt as if she was going to throw up. Her eyes felt like they were under fire and her vision was blurry. Her adrenaline was running high for a few minutes, then she suddenly became calm and focused.

"He's gonna die if you don't hurry the fuck up!" screamed Dayzee.

Five minutes later, they arrived, tires screeching, at the emergency room entrance.

'Ok, get you and this nigga out my shit!", yelled R'Mell.

"I'll go get someone! Talk to him until someone comes," said Dayzee.

"Hell naw! Get this muthafucka out my car, Day!! Shouted R'Mell.

Dayzee opened the passenger door and ran into the emergency room entrance as two nurses and a doctor ran out to the truck.

"What happened? Do you know his name?" asked the doctor as he checked Jay's pulse.

"No, we just saw him on the side of the road and brought him here", said R'Mell.

"Ok, thank you. Can you come in and make a statement?" said the officer who secretly opened her driver's side door.

"That's all I know. I don't know his name or what happened to him. You can ask my friend who was in the car too. She'll tell you the same thing", said R'Mell.

While all this was happening, R'Mell noticed Dayzee never came back out to the truck. She disappeared.

As R'Mell prepared to take off, the officer said, "Ma'am, can you step out of the car and put your hands behind your back?"

"Why? What did I do, officer?" says R'Mell in a monotone voice. R'Mell put the truck in park, pissed off.

"We need to ask you some questions", replied the officer.

R'Mell turned off the truck, opened her driver's side door, and got out with the officer placing her in handcuffs.

As R'Mell is being read her rights, she sees Dayzee on the skywalk looking down at her, smiling.

Imma kill that bitch, she thought.

Another officer joins the first officer. He starts looking through the truck and finds her purse.

"Let's see who you are," says the second officer.

"You're from Chicago, huh. Well, we do things differently here. Did you come here alone?" asks the officer as he tumbles through the truck, while the first officer just watched.

R'Mell stays silent. She could feel her blood boil. She wanted to cuss them out so badly, but she remembered Dre told her that her mouth would get them in trouble one day.

"Since you are being uncooperative, you're goin' downtown for questioning in this shooting", stated officer number two.

R'Mell didn't say a word. She kept her silence. All she could think about was Dre and how mad he was gonna be. That apartment was going to be the fresh start they came here for, and now she slipped up and let an old friend take that from them. The more she tried to put her old life behind her, the more she failed. Now she is gonna give the universe what it wants, the return of Blaque Butterfly.

Just Bad Luck

R'Mell could smell Skid Row coming through the small, barred window in the five-by-five cell hosted by the LAPD. Sirens in the distance give R'Mell thoughts of being back home in Chicago. Flashbacks of her old life, her new life, and runnin' into Dres's loving arms when she gets home. Images of Dre almost bring tears to her eyes. But with the life she chose, tears are shed only for the dead. Keepin' cool is what got her this far, and ain't no turning back now.

As R'Mell lights a Newport, she realizes their game has just begun. Life is about to get real, and the LAPD and D.A. ain't playing wit her ass this time. They got video, audio, and a living C.I. to hold her, they claim. Although the D.A. claims to have a witness, she knows she personally never leaves a witness. Plus, this is an accessory charge, for now. Nonetheless, she's wondering who this witness could be. No one can place her in what went down. It's been months, so *what witness?*

R'Mell inhales the last drag on her cigarette and tosses the butt in the silver porcelain god in the corner. As she turns from the window, she's annoyed by the keys of the C.O. coming down the hall. Keys jingling make the hair on the back of her neck stand at attention, along with her stomach queasy. They remind her of "him".

"Him." The one who took her innocence. The one who made her do things only a woman should do at six years old. Her mother's boyfriend, the asshole. R'Mell never says his name 'cause that would still give his dead ass power over her, and no man will ever have that much power over her ever again. She suppressed her childhood deep in the back of her mind years ago. There are still things, like the damn jingling of the C.O.'s keys, that trigger her. Those keys make the same noise as the ones that asshole wore coming home in his work boots. She could almost hear him come down the hall to her room as she hid, crying in her closet with the crystal doorknob. R'Mell used to be scared to death of him and hated visiting her mother in the summer. *He never made her sister do those nasty, perverted things, so "why me,"* she thought.

R'Mell put her past in a lockbox deep in her subconscious years ago, but with every negative situation in her life, memories and feelings creep back to the surface. She has a fear of abandonment, feelings of not being good enough, and low self-esteem. R'Mell's childhood trauma made a life-altering scar on her mindset. That is the reason she fell for Dre so quickly, because he was nothing like most men she had to deal with growing up. Dre actually loves and cares for her, and he has never abused her in any way, cheated, or lied to her. She trusts him with her life. Dre is the only man walking the earth who possesses power over her, and that power is love. Dre and family are the only people who can take her to another mindset. R'Mell chose to be in the frame of mind of leaving the street life and behaviors back in Chicago and focus on becoming a mother and career woman. However, since the tires touched California concrete, her street mindset has resurfaced. All she wants is to know what happiness feels like, more than anything. Maybe the street mentality is what she needs to keep for now to appreciate true happiness when God says it's time. God will test us until He feels we are ready for His blessings. Until then, R'Mell will do what needs to be done to keep them safe and eventually receive the life she deserves.

Get out ya head, Mell. You've got bigger problems now, she whispered to herself.

She started humming while she paced the floor of her cell to drown out the sound of those damn keys.

"Reeves, your lawyer is here", barked Officer Brown.

"My bail ain't posted yet? R'Mell shouted back through the bars.

"Hell naw! Turn your ass around and assume the position", shouted Officer Brown, approaching her cell.

If looks could kill, the ugly, black, heavy-set cop attempting to play his weak-ass authority would be outlined in chalk if he were on the street. R'Mell slaps her hands together, wishin' she could slap the taste out of his mouth for the disrespectful tone. As she gets up off the cement bed, she slowly turns and faces the barred window to walk backwards toward the cell door.

"Nigga, do you know who you talkin' to? You must be new or got a family death wish", replied R'Mell with anger in her tone.

Officer Brown grabbed R'Mell out of the cell by her long braids and slammed her face-first into the adjacent wall. With his forearm on the nape of her neck, he said, "Naw, bitch, and I don't give a fuck who you are! And threatening an officer will get you a first-class ride to solitary. But lookin' at that ass might make a nigga forget you even made that statement."

"Nigga, I would walk through hell wit gasoline draws on before I let you touch me", replied R'Mell as she struggled to free herself. "But I got a sweet pussy young hoe for ya, if you get me a roll of clean t.p.", she added.

With a Joker-looking smile, Officer Brown licked his lips and stated, "Yeah, ok", as he clicked the shackles on her small wrist, saying, "that bitch pussy better make me wanna leave my wife bitch. Like I said, yo lawyer here to see you". As he grabbed R'Mell by her hair, he forced her down the hallway to the lawyer's visiting room.

All the while, R'Mell is silently thinkin' of how she's gonna get this muthafucka murked. He wants to play cat and mouse, and she's got the perfect pussy for him. He either really doesn't know who he fuckin wit or doesn't give a fuck. Either way. *He'll never forget me,* she thought.

Officer Brown pushed her into the room, almost causing her to trip.

"Bitch ass nigga! Keep it up!" she shouted. Almost hitting the steel table in front of her.

"We'll see who the bitch is later", he replied.

"Officer, there's no need for your actions or bulllshit. Now, please remove these handcuffs and get out before I have YOU arrested for disorderly conduct against my client", said Attorney Johnson. As she stood up from the table and began to walk him out of the room, she continued, "You talkin' shit on my time now. Get out!"

"Fuck both y'all", he said, unlocking R'Mell's cuffs. Before he could finish and walk out, R'Mell stood from the table in front of him and said, "Nigga, if I ever hear you speak to my..." Attorney Johnson got between them and pushed Officer Brown out the room door and pointed for R'Mell to sit back down.

After Attorney Johnson checked the hallway to make sure the coast was clear, she closed the door and slowly sat down in front of R'Mell, who was tapping on the table to calm herself down.

Attorney Johnson crossed her legs to her navy Prada pant suit and looked R'Mell in the eyes, whispering, "You must want me to get thrown off your case. Do you?"

R'Mell rolled her eyes at her.

Attorney Johnson continued, "If you think you can come in here and act like you do on the streets, you got a rude awakening. This is some serious shit I got to get you out of. Pissin' off these officers is only gonna make yo visit harder. Now, are you gone work wit me on this shit or do you have a public pretender you deem more suitable?"

In a calm monotone voice, R'Mell states, "First of all, you gone stop raisin yo' voice at me like I'm the little sister. I'm six minutes older than you. Second, I don't give a fuck about no C.O., no P.O., and especially no D.A. Fuck all these acronym name havin' muthafuckas. I've been here almost 72 hours and they still ain't charged me yet. And finally, I pay yo ass good to be here when I need you. So shut the fuck up and tell me what you found out, Reese."

R'Mell and her sister grew up in the same house with the same parents, but took two different paths in life. When they were four, their parents divorced. Their mother, R'Shawn, took back her maiden name, Johnson, and moved R'Neece to Atlanta with her family. While their father, James Richards, stayed in L.A. with R'Mell. The girls would see each other during summer vacations and holidays, and when their older brother, Ray, came home from the military. Otherwise, they didn't share the same love and respect for each other as most fraternal twins.

Face to face, "My name is Attorney Johnson to you while I'm working, Mell, and no one can know we are related. The D.A. would request my removal from your case in a heartbeat", whispering Reese.

R'Mell sucked her teeth while staring at Reese with disgust.

"Are we gonna get down to tactics or are we gonna continue this played out sibling rivalry shit 'cause I got work to do", said Attorney Johnson.

R'Mell caved and shook her head. She knows she needs her sister's help, and fighting with her isn't going to get her out of jail any sooner. She needed to be back at Diamond and Chance's house, thinking of a new strategy on getting a job, and back in Dre's arms like yesterday. Plus, in the back of her mind, she knows it's getting close to Dre starting his new job. So, she just stared and listened.

As Attorney Johnson started talking, all R'Mell could think about was how much she really loves and respects Reese. Their childhood was so fucked up, and it drove them apart. Time will tell if she can actually get Reese to feel the same way about her. After all, they are and will always be sisters.

"The District Attorney's Office is charging you, as an accessory, with First Degree Intentional Homicide, Possession of a Firearm, AND Intimidation of a Witness. R'Mell, these are serious charges, so I need you to be completely honest with me and tell me what happened Friday night", said Attorney Johnson in a stern voice while staring at R'Mell.

"If I tell you what went down, you could be in danger", said R'Mell with sadness in her voice. R'Mell was staring at her fingers tapping on the table, thinking she didn't want her little sister in the middle of the lifestyle she chose. Losing Reese to bullshit would kill her and make her spill more blood on the streets of Los Angeles.

"Before I say anything about that bullshit, what proof do those assholes think they got on me?" R'Mell shouted for the C.O.'s eavesdropping in the hallway could hear her.

"I've been told by D.A. Spence that their office has a videotape from the apartment building and a telephone text of you conversing with C.I. Jay Lewis. They are using him as an eyewitness in the shooting. The deceased, "Beauty", whose real name is Walter Layton, had two pounds of heroin in the apartment where they found his body. The apartment was leased to the deceased, but the 9mm found next to his body wasn't. The apartment was clean except for an open window. They have Mr. Lewis in custody also, but he hasn't made a formal statement as of yet since being released from the hospital." Attorney Johnson got up from the table and started pacing the floor, tapping her pen against her cheek.

She started, "As I see the case right now, until Mr. Lewis gives his statement, all they have is hearsay, and you will be released in a few hours. You've been here 72 already, so they should be letting you go any minute or charging you. But Mr. Lewis has to talk", stated Attorney Johnson.

R'Mell smiled and said, "Dat nigga ain't gone talk cause he know what's up if he do. And as far as these bogus ass charges, they can kiss my big black ass! I'm not goin' down for no murder! You better find out what's the hold up on my release and get me the fuck outta here!" shouted R'Mell.

Attorney Johnson rubbed her forehead in confusion, but also sadness. She loves her big sister but wishes she didn't live the way she does. She chose the right path in life and can't understand why R'Mell made the choice not to follow her dreams. R'Mell graduated with a master's degree in business with Honors from the University of Chicago when she was only twenty-two years old. She had a bright future, but somehow staying involved with Dre changed all that. Attorney Johnson often wondered if she had lived with her and Momma, would R'Mell have chosen differently? Now look at the mess she's got them both in. The brightly lit stars glaring through the conference room window didn't give Attorney Johnson the answers she needed. She sighed and shook her head to herself, knowing this case wasn't going to be easy. Nonetheless, she had to give it her all because this is family, plus she wanted to make partner, and this type of case might just be the one to make that happen.

Snapping out of her daydream, she heard R'Mell shouting, "Bitch, do you hear what the fuck I'm sayin'? Do they have any fingerprints or DNA from the muthfuckin' apartment or not?"

As Attorney Johnson turned around to return to the table, she said, "Sorry, Mell. I was just thinking of how to proceed. I'm sorry, you were asking about fingerprints and DNA?"

While Attorney Johnson shuffled through her notes, mumbling to herself, R'Mell could tell that something was bothering her sister. So, she changed her attitude and touched her sister's hand and softly asked, "You o.k. Reese? What's up wit chu? You seem distracted."

"It's personal, Mell, and nothing we can discuss right now. I'm here to help you. I'll be fine." With tears welling up in her eyes, she couldn't tell her big sister what had happened to her because R'Mell would snap. Her situation will have to stay buried, for now.

Finally finding the Crime Scene Report, she stated, "No other fingerprints were found but Mr. Layton's; however, they found saliva on a blunt in an ashtray that was not the DNA of Mr. Layton. It was female. And the gun was wiped clean. So, as I said, they only have circumstantial evidence. Which means you should have already been released."

Attempting to change the subject, Attorney Johnson stated, "Mell, tell me what went down Friday night. I need to know before speaking with ADA Spence. I don't like surprises; you know that."

'Okay, but I need to tell you something, Reese", whispered R'Mell.

As R'Mell leaned into Attorney Johnson to speak, the conference room door flew open, and Officer Brown stepped in and shouted, "Times up, bitches! It's time for count. So, say your damn good nights and let's go, Ms. Reeves!"

R'Mell looked at Attorney Johnson with fire in her eyes and a blood taste in her mouth. *This nigga is really forcin' it,* she thought to herself. She balled up her fists and slammed them on the table before standing and turning around to give Officer Brown a knee in his balls that he'd never forget.

"Ugh! You lesbian bitch!" cried Officer Brown as he fell to the concrete floor in the fetal position.

Two other officers appeared and grabbed R'Mell by the arms, escorting her out of the conference room.

"I told you about talkin' to my attorney with disrespect muthafucka. You'll learn", said R'Mell as she spat on Officer

Brown, smiling as she was shoved out the door by the other two officers.

"Let's go, Ms. Reeves!" said Officer Hyde.

"I'll be back tomorrow afternoon, Ms. Reeves", shouted Attorney Johnson while laughing and shaking her head, looking at Officer Brown crying on the floor.

Attorney Johnson gathered her things and put them in her briefcase before closing it. She grabbed her coat from the back of her chair. Before leaving, she kneeled beside Officer Brown and said, "Who's the bitch now, fat boy?" She stood and closed the door behind her.

"Fuck you!" shouted Officer Brown.

As Dre stands on the balcony of his father's house, staring down the street at a blue Camaro that has been parked for hours, occupied. He is in beast mode, knowing he's being watched. But by whom? *Which wanna-be gangster is it today,* he wondered. He is used to it now, same shit, different day.

Dre was born on the streets of L.A. and knows the game. His parents were about that life and taught him well. After losing his father in a drive-by, Dre took his father's position and became the most wanted man in L.A. After his father's death, he had to maintain L.A. and South Chicago without R'Mell knowing. Now that she told him she has known for some time, he didn't have to pretend anymore. When he was in Chicago, Diamond and Chance took care of the house. When R'Mell gets back in L.A., he will bring her home. To his house, their house.

Dre pulled out his cellphone to call his security down the block. "Dub? Can you see a blue Camaro from yo' lookout point?, asked Dre.

"Naw! Were he at, bro?" asked Dub.

"Aight. If you see it pull off, I need a face and a plate nigga", Dre stated firmly and hung up.

Just as Dre was gonna sit down, he heard, "Uncle Dre, can I have some more cake?" asked Dayja.

"Yeah, go ahead, Day. But it better be a small piece. Your mother is on her way to get chu", said Dre with a smile.

"Okay!" said Dayja as she ran back in the house to the kitchen, where Darren was already slicing him a piece.

Dre could hear his niece and nephew in the kitchen arguing over how much bigger Darren's piece of cake was than Dayja's. He just laughed to himself and looked up Budlong for his sister, who is late getting off work again. He helps her with the kids since Chance is handlin that lick in Miami. He can't wait until next week when he gets back so he can have their house back.

Just as he was gonna go in the house to get Dayja off her brother's ass, Diamond pulled up blowin' the horn.

"Okay!" said Dre as he waved to signal he was walking the kids out. He checked his burner in his back to make sure he was ready in case he was just mistaken about the Camaro. He let the kids wrap up their cake and helped them gather all their stuff to get them out the door.

"I'm so sorry, bro. Traffic is crazy tonight. Everybody tryin' to get to the Laker game. Thank you. I love you!" said Diamond while helping the kids get settled in the car. Diamond looked out the passenger side window at Dre and noticed that he wasn't listening to her.

"Dre! Did you hear me? You okay?, asked Diamond, leaning over to the passenger seat to see Dre staring at something up the street.

Dre is staring down the street at the blue Camaro. He could see a lot of movement inside, and then someone was hanging out the back window. The car's lights suddenly turned on, and the car was headed toward them fast.

"Get down!" shouted Dre. Dre grabbed his .357 Magnum from his back waistband and ran out into the middle of the street. He started shooting out the windshield of the Camaro. The rear passenger returned fire with an AK-47. Dre ducked behind a cable van to return fire, but the Camaro hit the corner before he could get a good look at who was in the driver's seat. He got up and looked inside the van to notice the cable man slumped over the steering wheel with his face blown open.

Dre ran back to his sister's BMW, screaming, "Diamond! Diamond, y'all alright?

Diamond was half in the front seat and half in the back already screaming, "My babies! My babies!"

Dre looked in the back seat and noticed Darren also slumped over with a bullet hole in his left temple and one in his chest. "Darren! Darren! shouted Dre while noticing the gunshots in the rear door. He opened the door and saw the lifeless body of his nephew and a blood-stained yellow dress that Dayja was wearing.

Dre didn't want to accept what he was seeing; both his niece and nephew were gone. Suddenly, Dayja sat up. Dayja stared at Darren with a terrified gaze while Dre slowly grabbed Darren from his seat belt and placed him on the ground, screaming and crying. Diamond jumped out of the car and kneeled beside her son, screaming and crying so uncontrollably that all Dre could do was try to console her. Dayja was still in a tearful-eyed trance from what just happened, so she just sat in her seat without making a sound.

He's gone, Diamond, he's gone", Dre kept repeating to Diamond while hugging and rocking her. He could hear the police coming, so he got up and ran to hide his gun while also grabbing Dayja to take her back in the house.

Who in the fuck would be this bold to try to kill me in front of my family, he thought. After hiding the burner, he returned outside to find the police and ambulance standing over his nephew and sister.

"Ma'am, please let us tend to your son", asked a female EMT.

Dre held up his hand and motioned to the police officer and EMT to let him remove Diamond. "Diamond, let these people do their job and get Darren out of here. You have to be strong for Dayja now. She's scared and needs her mom. Come on, Diamond", whispering Dre while lifting Diamond up and out of the way.

"They killed my baby! What am I going to tell Chance, huh? Oh my God!" screamed Diamond. "Where's Dayja? Where's my baby girl?" she added while running into the house.

"Mommy!" yelled Dayja from the living room. She was surrounded by police detectives. Dayja ran into her mother's arms with kisses from Diamond. Dre walked into the living room, upset because he did not grant permission for the officers to enter his house.

"You have no authority to speak to my niece without her mother or lawyer present", stated Dre as he walked toward Defective Simmons.

Detective Simmons stood smiling toward Dre and said, "I wasn't questioning the child; just trying to talk to her so she feels safe. Especially with you around, Mr. Reeves."

Detective Carl Simmons has been trying to get anything on Dre and his family for years. Simmons and Dre grew up together, so they know each other like brothers. Their fathers were best friends in the game, so they were always together. Sadly, Carl's brother was killed when they were 16, and Carl feels Dre had him set up. Carl became a police officer when he got D.P.'d out of the gang and swore revenge. However, Dre knows where all his bodies are buried, so he knows he'd better tread lightly. That's why he acted as if he didn't know him at the hotel, plus he wasn't sure about R'Mell yet. Obviously, he now knows she is his wife. Now that this tragedy happened on his property, he thinks he finally has a case to build against him, so he doesn't have to keep the act going.

"Mr. Reeves, I need you and your sister to come downtown to give a statement. So, contact your crooked lawyer to have him meet you there. And bring bail money for your wife," smiled Detective Simmons as he walked away, shaking his head in amusement.

All Dre could do was stand there with his arms at his side and look stupid. He thought R'Mell was in Frisco for the weekend, shopping for new furniture. Now he has two fires to put out. What the hell did she do to get locked up this time, he thought. "Damn!" he shouted. Dre walked over to Diamond and told her he'll be back downstairs in a minute.

Dre climbs the stairs to his bedroom to get his coat and wallet to see police officers going through his things. He snapped. "Get the fuck out of my house! The crime happened outside, not in my house muthafuckas!" The crooked-ass L.A.P.D. will try it all to get a piece of him. "Get the fuck out!" he shouted and slammed his bedroom door.

Dre sat on his bed with his hands over his face in rage. He was so pissed off that he didn't hear Diamond and Dayja walk in.

Diamond sat down next to Dre and asked, "Dre, what do I say when we get downtown?"

"You tell them the truth on this one. We are the victims here. Criminal justice for Darren is what this case will be about. I will personally attend to the street justice myself", stated Dre. With tears in her eyes, Diamond shook her head and kissed him on the forehead. Dre grabbed her hand and looked her in the eyes and said, "I promise, sis."

Diamond stood and softly grabbed Dayja by the shoulders and led her out of the room. Dayja ran back to Dre and hugged him around the neck. "I love you, Uncle Dre."

"I love you too, Dayja", said Dre. He kissed her forehead, and she ran to Diamond, who shut the door behind her.

Dre sat in a blood thirsty rage. He had an idea of who may have put the green light on him, but that has to be put on the back burner for now. He has to figure out what he's going to tell these assholes downtown and get R'Mell out of jail. He grabs his wallet and coat and heads downtown for another long night of bullshit with the L.A.P.D.

* * * * *

Attorney Johnson was listening to her voicemails and heard an anxious call from Dre saying to get downtown right away.

"What now?" she cried. She was still in the county jail parking lot after dealing with R'Mell.

She returned Dres' call, and he filled her in on what happened. All she could do was put her forehead on her steering wheel and cry. Her nephew was now gone due to the lifestyle that Dre and R'Mell led. Another innocent child; taken way too soon. She told Dre that she hadn't left the jail yet and had just gotten finished filing paperwork to get R'Mell released. "I'll wait for you in the lobby", she said and hung up in frustration.

Dre and Diamond walked in, and Attorney Johnson embraced them both. "I'm deeply sorry for your loss, Diamond. Keep your answers brief and only answer if I say it's okay to. Got it?" asked Attorney Johnson to Diamond. Diamond shook her head yes and then sat down with Dayja on the lobby room bench.

The precinct smelled of lies and corruption. Officers walked around as if the world revolved around them, while citizens pleaded to speak to someone. The lobby was filled with people either paying tickets at the kiosk or sitting in frustration waiting to be called by a detective for some bullshit statement.

"You know the drill, Dre. I'm telling you to play the game. These muthafuckas want you behind bars and have already tried R'Mell and found that was a bad idea. Keep calm, and I'll take care of this. We clear?" asked Attorney Johnson sternly while staring straight into Dres's eyes.

Taking a deep breath, Dre said, "Crystal. Let's get this shit over with." They both started walking toward the desk when Dre asked, "Where's Mell?" Attorney Johnson replied, "Let's deal with this first, Dre."

Standing in front of the Intake window, the youthful officer smiled and asked Attorney Johnson, "How may I help you, Attorney Johnson?"

Attorney Johnson replied, "My clients, Mr. Reeves and Ms. Clark, are here to give their statements. Detective Simmons is expecting us."

"Okay. I'll let him know you are here. Have a seat; it'll be just a few moments," stated the young officer.

"Thank you", stated Attorney Johnson with a smile. Dre sat next to Diamond and held her. She had started to cry again.

Attorney Johnson walked toward Dayja and kneeled in front of her. "You ok, Day?" she asked. Dayja was sitting, playing with her ponytail, and just staring into space. When Dayja noticed her, she snapped out of her trance and smiled to say, "Yeah, Auntie Reesee, I'm ok. Mommy is crying again. Why did the man in the blue car kill my brother?"

"I don't know, sweetheart, but Uncle Dre, your mommy, and I are here to talk to the police to find out, ok", said Attorney Johnson while smiling and stroking Dayja's hair as she sat down next to her. Attorney Johnson knew she had her hands full. She couldn't believe R'Mell was in jail, her innocent nephew was dead, and she had a separate murder trial starting in the morning. Looking at the clock on the wall behind the intake station, Attorney Johnson realized she had been awake for twenty-nine hours. With a screaming headache in her hands, she lifted her head at the call of her name.

"Attorney Johnson", shouted the young officer. Attorney Johnson slowly turned to look in the officers' direction, and the officer waved at her to come to the desk. That head-bangin' headache had her seeing stars. When she stood, Dre jumped up to catch her from tilting onto the bench she was sharing with Dayja.

"Woo!, said Attorney Johnson, feeling woozy when she stood holding her head in pain.

"I got chu, Reese, I got chu", said Dre while holding Attorney Johnson's right arm.

"Thanks, bro. I'm ok", laughed Attorney Johnson while grabbing her portfolio and purse.

Walking toward the station, Attorney Johnson says, "Yes. Are we ready?"

"Detective Simmons has been called out on a call and requests that you and your clients return at 7 a.m. tomorrow to give their statements. He apologizes for the inconvenience and will bring breakfast", smiled the young officer.

Irritated, Dre walks up to the station yelling about how he has been waiting for over an hour and wants to give his statement now 'cause he has to be at work at 7 a.m. *This lyin' ass nigga know he don't have no damn job!,* thought Attorney Johnson not knowing he does have a new job. Diamond grabbed Dayja from the bench and started walking out the front door, shouting "Let's just go" at Dre. Dre was still shouting and not even paying attention to Diamond. Diamond sucked her teeth, pushed Dayja out the double doors, and left.

Tired of hearing Dre complain about his precious time, Attorney Johnson finally spoke out of exhaustion. Squeezing Dre's arm hard enough to leave a bullfrog, she looked at him and said, "Dre, let me handle this." Pushing Dre to the closed side of the intake window, she looked at the eager young officer and calmly stated, "We have quietly and patiently waited for over an hour for my clients to give their statements. So now that we have been inconvenienced, please let Detective Simmons know that I am in trial for the remainder of the week. My clients have prior engagements and cannot make his requested return day or time." Raising her voice so that other police personnel would hear. "So, inform Detective Simmons that neither my clients nor I are available in the morning, so he will wait for me to find time to escort my clients back to this shit hole. He knows how to reach me. Have a nice damn day." Attorney Johnson stormed out of the station, pissed and tired, toward her car, not hearing little Dayja saying goodbye.

Still in shock, Dre and the young officer look at each other and laughed. Dre was confused but relieved Reese snapped out instead of him. "Is she ok?" asked the young officer.

Staring in awe at the front station door, Dre replied, "Hell, I don't know." Coming out of shock, Dre looked at the young, pretty officer with a smile and said, "I need to know when R'Mell Reeves will be released."

The young officer shrugged her shoulders at Dre. His poor act of being charming wasn't working on her. Everyone in L.A. knows who Dre and R'Mell are. Dre is fine, but *he ain't worth losing a job or a life for*, she thought. Maybe his poor act could be useful at a later time.

The young officer returned a flirtatious smile and said, "Ms. Reeves' paperwork is being processed, so she should be ready in a few hours."

"Thank you", stated Dre. Pondering his next move, he walked toward Diamond and Dayja, waiting outside. Standing at the door, Dre wondered if he should wait for R'Mell to get released or just send Tank back to scoop her. Dre pulled out his cellphone and called Tank. "Tank, come sit at the jail and wait on Mell. She should be ready in a couple hours." Dre walked through the double doors and told Diamond, "Come on, let me take y'all home."

He put on his Gucci shades, and they started toward his car when he heard "Dre!" come from behind him. Frustrated, Dre stopped, took off his shades, and slowly turned to see Ray smiling back at him.

Dre told Diamond to get in the car. *Where the hell...*, thought Dre as he returned a smile out of confusion. "What up, nigga!" he shouted. Walking up to Ray and giving him dap, Dre shouts with laughter, "Where the fuck you come from?"

Ray daps and hugs Dre and says, "Nigga! I just got off the Chino Limo. Processing out and ready to get the fuck away from this muthafucka, man! The question is, who are you here for? Mell or yo 'self, nigga?, asks Ray with laughter. Dre laughs as he starts walking toward his car again.

"Hey, was that Diamond? Asked Ray, pointing at Diamond as she put Dayja in the back seat of Dre's car and then got in herself without saying hello.

Ray is Dre's brother-in-law. Dre has only known Ray for the past couple of years because he was in the military when he and R'Mell met. They are cordial towards each other, at best. Ray always felt his baby sister deserved better than Dre. He wanted R'Mell to be with one of those proper talkin' niggas' that she used to know in college.

"Neither. I'm down here with my sister handling some business", replied Dre with the fakest smile he could muster. Walking faster away from Ray, Dre yelled, "Aight, Ray. I'm a holla at chu later, bro!" Dre didn't even turn around to see if Ray heard him or not. He jumped in his car and sped off. Dre just didn't have anything left to entertain Ray. All he wanted to do was get home before R'Mell and to give her a proper welcome home. *"Fuck dat nigga"*, whispered to himself. Dre calls Chance and tells him to meet him at the spot at 7 tonight. "Ray's back in town. Get the council and the ladies assembled for a meeting tomorrow night. When he's in town, that means only one thing", stated Dre as he hung up the phone. He didn't mention what happened to Darren. He needed him to think it was about business, so he wouldn't flip out, finishing up in Mexico.

Ray knows Dre is lying 'cause the C.O. on the ride downtown already let him know R'Mell was locked up. Plus, he already knew. He was informed after she was arrested a few days ago; another mess he gotta clean up. He feels sorry for Dre 'cause he knows his life is getting ready to be turned upside down. As he watches Dre speed off, his phone rings.

"Yeah", answers Ray to the caller. Throwing up the peace sign as Dre speeds away, he states, "He just left". Turning into the lobby of the police station, Ray says, "I won't fail you," and hangs up.

The Boss in The Lion's Den

The sun over Michoacán didn't rise; it radiates. It bled across the Sierra Madre peaks, spilling gold over the terra-cotta tiles of the Garcia estate. Miguel Garcia stood on his balcony, the smoke from his Cohiba curling into the crisp morning air. From this height, he could see the perimeter. Armed men in tactical gear patrolling the bougainvillea-lined walls, their shadows long and sharp.

In Chicago, Miguel was a ghost, a name whispered in back alleys. Here, he was a god.

He turned back into the cool, marble-floored bedroom. His house was a fortress of Spanish colonial elegance with arched doorways, hand-carved mahogany furniture, and religious icons draped in gold leaf. It was a place built on the blood of the "game," yet it smelled of jasmine and expensive wax.

He descended the grand staircase. At the head of a long, obsidian dining table sat a spread that looked more like a mural than a meal. Fresh papaya, pan dulce, and coffee so strong it could wake the dead.

Upstairs, Alexis checks herself in her full-length mirror one last time before heading downstairs for breakfast with her father. She is already late and knows how her father is a stickler for punctuality. The all-white Prada fit she is wearing must be right for her flight, or she will feel uncomfortable and ugly. She has to look and feel like money! Suddenly, she hears Bonita calling her in the distance, "Miss Alexis, your father requests you for breakfast", shouting through her bedroom door. Applying her mascara and singing as if she couldn't care less, she sniffs a line of coke and answers sarcastically, "Just make sure Ramon is dressed, Bonita. I'll be down in a minute, O.K." Alexis is excited this morning 'cause she's going back to the states on family business. While in Los Angeles, she also has plans to find and reconnect with the love of her life and the man her father and brother despise. She knows she'll have to be discreet in her plan, but she knows how to handle her father and brother. Alexis blows herself a kiss in the mirror and adjusts her double D twins and sighs at Bonita's voice saying, "Ms. Alexis, your father says NOW!"

"I heard you, you old bat! I'm coming! Damn, shouted Alexis.

Alexis grabbed her white mink Prada purse and the plate with her Coke on it. She placed her Coke in her wall safe behind her Starry Night painting and locked it. She then grabbed her matching jacket and swung open her bedroom door to find Bonita standing there looking stupid.

"You can bring down my luggage. Don't touch any of my shit, either," barked Alexis as she pushed past Bonita, rolling her eyes at her.

"Yes, ma'am, replied Bonita. "Spoiled bitch", Bonita said softly under her breath.

Alexis walked slowly down the winding staircase to see what position her father was in at the table. If he were just sitting there looking out the window into the garden, drinking coffee, he would be in a good mood. However, if he is reading the newspaper with it covering his face, he is upset and all about business. As she got further down the stairs into the view of the dining area, she could see him sitting at the table. All she could see was the front page of the New York Times and the steam from his coffee cup. Alexis paused, took a deep sigh, and descended into the unknown.

"Buenos Dias, Poppi," smiled Alexis, kissing her father on the cheek.
Before she could sit down, "Why are you late for breakfast, Hija? I don't have time to wait for you to finish putting on mascara and snorting your coke. When I say 7 a.m. I mean 7 a.m. NOT fucking 7:25 a.m.! shouted Miguel. "Do you understand hija?, calmly asked Miguel.

Feeling like a five-year-old child, no high left and scared as fuck, all Alexis could do was sit there and not move a muscle. Her father is a very powerful man; he's a Mexican drug lord. Others do what he says at the sound of his voice with no hesitation, or know they are dead. He's been in "business" before she was born, so he has major respect and power across the globe. Consuela, her birth mother, died in a car accident when she was just six years old. Ever since, it's just been her, her brothers, and her father. All of the children went to boarding schools and college, with Alexis being the youngest and the only girl.

Miguel Garcia has been in the game since he wore cloth diapers back in 1945. Miquel Garcia Sr. was also a powerful "business" man, and his mother was an heiress of a hotel mogul. They were both from Tijuana and married for over sixty years. Alexis' grandparents have passed on; they left an empire to her father to be kept in the family, and her father tends to keep it that way. There is no room for errors or laziness in the eyes of Miguel Garcia when it comes to the "family business". According to Alexis, no room for a life either. All she can do is what she is told, nothing outside of that. What her father says goes. He means well, but means fucking business. Miguel has many people working for him, but he trusted those who betrayed him, so he has become very cautious and devious over the years. No one but family knows the family business, and disloyalty is NOT TOLERATED. Disloyal people are terminated. Completely. Miguel Garcia can be a man with a heart of gold, but betray him and his heart turns to coal. Right now, she wants to remind him she is his only daughter.

"Yes, Poppi", softly replies Alexis with her head down

in her lap.

Her father is leaning forward in his chair, staring at her the whole time as if he is scolding a five-year-old child. Suddenly running into the breakfast nook yelling, "Mommy, I'm ready!, is Alexis' son, Raymone. Hello, Granddad."

Startled out of his stare, Miguel replied, "Well, good morning, grandson. Are you ready to go on your trip today? Miguel lifted Raymone onto his lap and kissed his forehead. The boy looked up, oblivious to the fact that his grandfather's hands had ordered the disappearance of dozens. Miguel watched him with a pride that didn't touch his heart, but rather his sense of ownership. This boy was the future of the Garcia name—a name Miguel had spent sixty years keeping at the top of the food chain.

"Yes, grandfather. I'm going on an airplane to Los Angeles," replied Raymone with excitement.

"Los Angeles", corrected Miguel, laughing.

Alexis is looking on, smiling.

"Oh, okay, grandfather. I'm gonna miss you, and I'm gonna call you every day", says Raymone while giving Miguel a good-bye hug and kiss.

"Okay, grandson. I will miss you too. I love you. Have a fun trip", replies Miguel.

"Love you too, grandfather", says Raymone as he's running out of the breakfast nook toward Bonita, who's standing in the rotunda.

Miguel turns his loving smile off like a light switch when he looks back at Alexis. Alexis' whole body stiffens in fear. Miguel folds his hands on the table in front of him and leans toward Alexis. His expression hardened. She was still sitting there, her head bowed in that performative submission he demanded. He knew she was high. He could see the slight tremor in her fingers, the way her pupils were swallowed by the dark iris. It disgusted him, not because of the drug itself—Miguel had built a kingdom on the habits of others—but because of the lack of control.

"You look at me when I speak, Hija," he commanded softly.

Alexis lifted her head, her jaw tight. "Yes, Poppi."

"I am sending you to Los Angeles not just to find that boy, Ray, but to remind the city who holds the leash," Miguel stated, his rings clinking against his coffee cup.

"Los Angeles is different from here. It's a hive. R'Mell and that man of hers... they think they've found a sanctuary in the sun. They think the distance from Chicago bought them a new life."

Alexis tore a piece of bread, her gaze steady. "They're wrong."

"Make sure they know how wrong they are," Miguel said. "Handle the family business, Alexis. Bring back what belongs to us. And if R'Mell stands in the way..." He paused, the smoke from his cigar drifting between them. "Remind her why butterflies shouldn't fly too close to a flame."

Alexis nodded, a cold smile playing on her lips. She didn't need a lecture on loyalty. She was her father's daughter, and Los Angeles was about to find out exactly what that meant.

Miguel stood up, signaling the end of the meal. "Bonita will travel with you. She will watch the boy while you handle the street work. I expect a call when you land. And Alexis..."

He paused at the door, silhouetted against the bright Mexican sun, and stated, "Do not let your feelings for that boy cloud your judgment again. I let you keep your son, don't make me take away a daughter."

Alexis felt a chill even the Mexican sun couldn't touch. She watched Miguel walk away, unbothered by his words. She reached for her Prada bag, her fingers brushing the cold steel of the gun she'd hidden there.

With her eyes still on the back of her father's head, Alexis barked, "Bonita, get the bags. We're leaving."

She stood from the table and walked toward the rotunda where Bonita and Raymone were waiting. She wished she had put another hit in her purse.

Alexis couldn't help thinking of her mission at hand. She knows what is expected of her, but she has a mission of her own to see through. Too much time has gone by, and her life has been put on hold. Getting her family back together is just as important to her as the family business, but her father wouldn't understand that. That's why she has to do things her way, secretly, and this business trip gives her the proper time and opportunity to handle her business as well.

'Ms. Alexis!" yells Bonita. "The car is here!" Alexis didn't hear Bonita while deep in thought. "Okay, Bonita. You don't have to yell. I heard you," barked Alexis, too embarrassed to say she wasn't paying attention.

"Come on, Raymone", says Bonita to get Raymone to come from playing with his cars in the rotunda. The maids and Bonita packed the luggage in the car while the armed guards stood watch, while Alexis and Raymone entered the bulletproof limo. Before the driver was allowed to drive off, two of the guards checked the car and then gave him a nod of approval to proceed. Raymone could be seen waving goodbye to the staff from the back window. When Alexis turned around, she saw her father also standing in the rotunda with his hands in his pockets. He then pulled out his cell phone and began talking, and then he was out of sight.

"Sit down, hijo", requested Alexis. Raymone turned around to sit down and put on his headphones to play his Nintendo. Alexis stared out the window, contemplating which step on her list to start with once she hits Los Angeles. Her list or the family business? Which is more important?

Suddenly, Alexis's cell phone rang. It's her brother, Alex.

"I guess this answers my questions", she whispers to herself.

"Hola hermano," said Alexis, annoyed.

"English, please. Have you left yet? You have a 3:00 appointment already set up with the loan officer," stated Alex. Alex is her older brother by two minutes. Alexis has deep green eyes, while Alex has deep blue. They share jet black hair and their mother's smile. Alex is just like his father when it comes to the family business. He lives in Los Angeles to stay next to business there. However, he travels to New York and Dallas twice a month. With a master's degree in business from USC, he thinks he knows everything and doesn't know shit. His wife, Maria, is the daughter of one of Miguel's friends who thinks he's a god. Little does anyone know, he is nothing but a common criminal in a business suit.

"I'm heading to the jet as we speak", claimed Alexis.

"Remember what's at stake. We need this to go down without any problems; this has to go down without a hitch, Lexi", shouted Alex.

"I know, Lex. I understand how important this is for the family business. I won't let you or father down", said Alexis. While she takes a look down and smiles at Ramone, who's playing his Nintendo, she turns to the window and whispers, "Did you do what I asked of you?" asks Alexis.

"He was let out this morning, and he's staying at the Western Motel on Vermont. Do not, I repeat, do not see him before our business is through. I need your head in the business," said Alex.

"I promise. Thanks, Lex. I'm at the jet. See you soon," she said as she hit end on her phone.

Ramone, still engulfed in his Nintendo, didn't even notice they were at the jet already.

"Let's go, mijo. Let's go see daddy."

On to Business

"Reeves! You got cho' walkin' papers. Let's go!" said Officer Brown, walking down the hall, dangling his keys. The sun was already beaming through the bars of R'Mell's cell, so it had to be a little after six in the morning. She was standing at the sink brushing her teeth when she heard the gorilla growling. She'd been waiting damn near a week on them to let her go. R'Mell turned to face the ugly beast as he was screaming, "Unlock cell 12". Wiping her mouth with a washcloth, R'Mell stated, "Fatboy, you better not be on no bullshit this early in the damn mornin', cause I ain't no mornin' bitch. You feel me?" Officer Brown replied so close to R'Mell's face she could spell the glazed donuts on his breath.

"Bitch, grab yo shit so you can get yo funky ass off my cell block. And if you ever come back, I will personally welcome yo black sexy ass with open arms (grabbing his gun holster). Now let's go."

R'Mell grabbed her journal and cigarettes and stood in front of Officer Brown and said, "Then lead the way, you black, fat, ugly muthafucka." R'Mell then laughed as Officer Brown placed handcuffs on her wrists. They were playing mouse with their eyes as he tightened the handcuffs with force and smirked. The handcuffs were so tight R'Mell had to bite her tongue in pain so he wouldn't get a hard on knowing he'd hurt her. Another C.O. was waiting outside the cell and stated, "Move out." R'Mell took one last look behind her to make sure she had all her shit before she exited the cell.

Once R'Mell received her personal belongings, she made a call on her cell. "Staci, I'm ready. And don't pick me up in the Lady, she stated before hanging up.
Two days ago, Diamond came to see R'Mell in jail. She said she took off from work early to come talk to her while Dre had the kids. With Chance being out of town, she needed to talk to her alone. Diamond led off the conversation by explaining that Chance filled her in on what happened in Chicago and provided a new position for R'Mell. R'Mell agreed to the new arrangement, but a piece of her died inside that she couldn't show. Her whole body felt numb, and she had to muster every ounce of strength she had left not to cry in front of Diamond. This new arrangement was going to take her mind back to a place she was trying to get away from. Twenty minutes later, the black Escalade she told Staci not to pick her up in rolled up in front of the jail. R'Mell shook her head in disgust and whispered to herself, " *This is a stupid as bitch*". Just then, Staci jumps out of the passenger seat screamin, "I know, I know, I know" while opening the rear door for R'Mell to get in.

"Tina had to make the Lillie's drop off in the Benz, so Dee was only left with the Lady", explained Staci with uncertainty in her voice. "Plus, we weren't expecting to pick you up until this afternoon".

"Shut up and get in the car", R'Mell replied. R'Mell gets in, and Staci closes the door behind her, smacking her teeth. In the car is the driver, Dee, who is R'Mell's left hand, Staci, who is her security, and Jazz, who does whatever needs to be done.

"What's up, Dee, Jazz?" said R'Mell.

"You boss lady!" they simultaneously respond. Diamond has a tight operation, and now that R'Mell is in charge of them, she will show Dre' and L.A. what she is capable of.

"All I can say right now is I'm out that dusty muthafucka! Now, I want to make some rounds, get my plate, and get to my dick. In that exact muthafuckin order. Any questions?"

R'Mell didn't wait for an answer, shouting, "So let's move."

Her new crew laughs while Dee pushes play on the dashboard and pulls out of the parking lot, headed to the 105 Freeway. Jazz is almost finished rolling the first of many blunts that will be placed in rotation while R'Mell sits back and smells the funk of her city's life. Jazz hands her a fat blunt and says, "This is for the queen only. Welcome home, boss lady." R'Mell takes the blunt into her mouth, Jazz lights it for her, and the first hit feels like silk gliding in and out of her throat. She cracks her window, leans her head back, and finishes her peach mango

Kush in silence, while enjoying the muggy air on her caramel-colored skin and the sounds of L.A. traffic.

How four days locked down can make you appreciate the little things you take for granted every day, she thought.

"Denker or Crenshaw, boss lady?" asked Dee.

"Denker. Let me out on 104th, I'm a walk", replied R'Mell.

Everyone looked at each other as if R'Mell had lost her mind. Jazz grabbed a full clip, knowin' R'Mell is losing her mind.

"Uh, boss lady, that's not a safe move", said Staci. Looking at Jazz for back-up.

"Bitch, that's why y'all heffa's are walkin too, shit", replied R'Mell.

"Glad I still got on my flats", laughed Jazz.

"Oh, shut up, Jazz", stated Staci.

"Ain't nobody tell yo ass not to go home after fuckin last night, bitch. You should have some extra clothes at that nigga house by now. Hell, you been fuckin' 'em long enough", laughed Dee and Jazz.

"Fuck y'all!" yelled Staci.

"Staci, you tellin' me you fuckin a nigga and he ain't let you leave an extra set of draws at his place or gave up a stack to buy you something else to wear home after he done stained yo shit up? Come on, I thought I taught you better than that", said R'Mell while laughing and shaking her head.

Rolling her eyes, Staci turned toward her friends and admitted, "He don't have his own place. He lives with his mother."

All the ladies chimed and laughed, "Aww, hell naw!"

"Fuck y'all! No disrespect, boss lady," yelled Staci.

"None taken. This some funny, sad shit in my book. We gone have an open class fo yo ass 'cause you a long way from boss bitch status. You way better at yo day job, boo," replied R'Mell.

"Alright, ladies, we've had our entertainment for the day, now let's get down to biz-ness!" stated R'Mell as the truck came to a halt.

Staci jumps out to check the block before opening the door for R'Mell. Jazz locks and loads the 9mm while Dee pops a clip in the Uzi before R'Mell exits the car. R'Mell changes from the fashionable county orange to her signature red bottoms, jeans, and white tee.

"Uh, where are my shades?" shouted R'Mell. Dee reached back into the Lady to the glove compartment and retrieved R'Mell's favorite Gucci shades and said, "Girl, right here. Don't have a baby!"

R'Mell snatched her shades and stated, "Bitch, don't be wishin' bad juju on me 'cause you gone take care of business if I do". And slammed the door.

"Hmm, hell if I do," replied Dee.

R'Mell started walking down Denker Avenue. It was a hot Saturday morning; still quiet, but people were out. She got to 102nd and saw the esse' sitting under his umbrella with his fruit stand. R'Mell made eye contact and the esse' gave her a nod. She looked at Jazz and Jazz said, "I got it." A half block up the street she made eye contact with Reverend Thomas and Sister Tate and they both gave a nod. Staci said, "I got it." All the children at the day care screamed "Hi Ms. R'Mell" from the playground. R'Mell crossed the street and gave Sister Tate $100 and told her to make sure they buy all the children new bibles and cases for bible school. Sister Tate thanked R'Mell with a hug and took the children inside for lunch. She waved goodbye to the children wondering to herself if she would ever be blessed with one of her own someday.

Loud music from behind her startled her out of her daydream. She turned to see Staci standing in front of her and Jazz by her side staring at a Hispanic man picking up his son from choir rehearsal across the street.

"Come on, let's keep moving", said R'Mell.

Down the next block, R'Mell made eye contact with the mailman, who also gave "the nod".

"Staci", R'Mell said softly.

"Already on it", replied Staci as she had her cellphone to her ear.

R'Mell turned to see a cream-colored limousine approach. Jazz was on point. "Stand down. I recognize this car," shocked and in disbelief, R'Mell changes her attitude and character to see Mrs. Lopez get out. Mrs. Lopez is a client she has been working with to seal a major investment deal for her father's firm back in Chicago. *But what was she doing in L.A. and how did she find me*, thought R'Mell.

"Mrs. Lopez, I thought I recognized your car. How are you today, and what brings you to Los Angeles?", smiling uncomfortably at her.

"Hello, Mrs. Reeves. Very nice to see you out here securing the site we have proposed. It looks like it's coming along just fine", stated Mrs. Lopez while looking out the corner of her eye at Jazz.

R'Mell didn't realize she was across the street from the site her father told her about a couple of weeks ago until Mrs. Lopez mentioned it. She had forgotten all about the deal. R'Mell wondered if her father was here in L.A.

"I just came out to speak to the foreman about budgeting and time frame so that we keep things in motion toward our deadline. Just formalities, you know," explained R'Mell in her professional voice.

"Yes, I understand, and it is refreshing to see you out in the field on such a hot day. Keep me posted. I'll see you next week. Chow for now", said Mrs. Lopez as she got back into her chauffeured limo.

R'Mell smiled and waved into the black-tinted windows as the limo pulled away.

"Fuck. That bitch caught me off guard. Now I must go and make sure this project goes smoothly," shouted R'Mell.

While reaching into her back pocket to retrieve her cellphone, it started ringing. It was her father.

"I need a minute, Jazz. Watch my back," said R'Mell to Jazz as she walked across the street toward the foreman standing in the field, smiling at her.

"Hi daddy" said R'Mell with a fake smile. R'Mell stopped in her tracks as he began to speak, wondering how he managed to call her at this exact moment. *Something is off.* She could feel it in her soul. It's the same childhood instinct of fear as soon as she stepped into her mother's house as a child.

"Hey, Mell. Just wanted to give you a heads up that Mrs. Cruz is in town and wanted to see the progress on the building. Talk to the foreman and make sure we're on schedule. I'll call you back," barked her father and hung up. R'Mell stood still, confused and paranoid.

"How the hell did he know I am in L.A. and that I just happened to be in front of the site? What the fuck is going

105

on?" R'Mell whispered to herself. Just then, the foreman waved her over. Waving at him, she looked back at Jazz to follow her. Walking toward the foreman, she looked at him with fire in her eyes and a smile, knowing that she and Dre had been found.

R'Mell spoke to the foreman as Jazz watched closely. Then they began to walk up Denker.

As they reached Century Boulevard, R'Mell could see Dee pulling up. Jazz and Staci got in. R'Mell shook the foreman's dirty hand and started walking across Denker Street. Suddenly, a black Benz with dark colored tinted windows and a blinged-out license plate with A.G. initialed, almost hit her. She came to a complete stop, touching the revving engine. She looked to see who the driver was so she could cuss him the fuck out. She reached for her pistol in the back of her shirt when she realized she was still in front of the school.

She stared into the car for it seemed like five minutes. The driver revved the engine once more. R'Mell slammed her hands on the hood of the Benz and raised her hands in the air, "What the hell!" Looking over at Sister Tate, she was heated in the moment. Is this nigga tryin to kill me, or is this nigga on a death wish to taunt me? She can't come out of character with so many people looking at her.

There was no response from the driver, so she continued across the street. The driver of the Benz waited until she crossed and pulled off, burning rubber. R'Mell looked at the Benz when she got in and didn't think any more of it.

"I have to check in on Daisy at the inn before I get my plate, Dee," said R'Mell nervously. Deep inside, R'Mell was shaken because she followed Diamond's instructions, and her timing was on point. It was a perfect scoop, but with too much extra, spontaneous bullshit.

"Okay, on our way," replied Dee.

"Jazz, call in my plate. Tell them to have it ready in 30 minutes," requested R'Mell.

"Yes, ma'am", replied Jazz.

"Staci, April on her way?" asked R'Mell.

"Yeah, she at the post office now and will meet us at the house in an hour", stated Staci.

"Good. Everything's running like clockwork. Give me the envelopes," stated R'Mell.

R'Mell counted and divided the money by the time she was in front of the blue door at the Inn.

"Call her ass and tell her to open the damn door!" R'Mell shouted.

"Day, open the door", said Jazz as she hung up the phone.

The blue door marked number eight swings open, and R'Mell says, "Let's go, Staci. Dee keep this muthafucka runnin' and Jazz, be Dee's second set of eyes. If we ain't out in exactly five minutes, Jazz come in blazin'. You feel me?"

Jazz replied, "I got chu."

Staci jumps out of the Lady and opens R'Mell's door and closes her own. R'Mell stands to the side while Staci closes her door. She walks toward number eight with Staci on her heels.

Upon entering the smoke-filled room, Daisy closes the door half-naked. The room has three other people in it: two men and one woman. They look like they haven't showered in days, and as high as the heavens.

"What's up, cuz! Glad to see they freed yo ass", said Daisy.

Daisy is R'Mell's first cousin and an on again off again crack head which explains her slim build and sunken eyes. She'll be clean for about six months, and then she relapses. She keeps business going because she doesn't get her product from Diamond. R'Mell loves her because she reminds her of her mother; they look just alike. Her aunt used to say that R'Mell's mother got on her nerves so much that Daisy came out lookin' just like her. And she was right. Daisy knew that by looking like her aunt, she made R'Mell uncomfortable looking at her in the eyes. They both have the same hazel eyes. They both came a long way from their childhood, and their sisterhood can never be broken.

"Yeah, I'm good. How's business?, says R'Mell as she scopes the room to see smokers all around her. She didn't have time for ideal chit-chat. She still has to eat and get home to ride Dre, so her time is priceless.

"Business is good, cuz. Lillie over there holdin' it down. We're gonna need a new washer soon, though. She riggin' it for now, but you know she workin' the shit out of it", stated Daisy.

"Alright. Hit Dee with the details by noon tomorrow so we can get it on order by next week. I'm here to collect right now, though," says R'Mell.

"Two minutes", says Staci as she looks at her watch.

"What?" says Daisy, looking confused at Staci.

Staci rolls her eyes at Daisy. They never saw eye to eye anyway.

"Nothing, Daisy. I just need my money", shouted R'Mell as she noticed the tension between the two.

"Oh, pink duffle bag by the door, cuz," says Daisy while still looking at Staci in confusion.

R'Mell grabs the bag on the way out the door. As she opens the door, Jazz is standing there ready to air it out. R' Mell points her to the car and looks back at Daisy and says, "Next week, same time, cuz. And don't forget to call Dee tomorrow. Love."

Staci closed the blue door while Daisy was still standing in it. She reaches the truck to open R'Mell's door for her to get in and immediately hops in through her passenger side door.

"That was close as fuck!" shouted Staci.

"You said five minutes, boss", says Jazz.

Dee's staring at R'Mell through the rear-view mirror, and R'Mell says, "Let's go get tatted, Dee."

All in unison, everyone said, "Tatted?"

"Yeah, bitches I said tatted. You got a problem wit that?" yelled R'Mell.

No one said a word as Dee drove to the tattoo shop on Fig. Two hours later, they were laughing at the tatts they got. It was a black butterfly on their right shoulder.

R'Mell started, "Alright, ladies, now that we all have a badge of honor, let's go eat."

Without saying a word to anyone, R'Mell notices the black car that almost ran over her following them. *It's probably nothing. I'm being paranoid'*, she thought.

Dee pulls out of the parking lot and heads down Century Boulevard toward R'Mell's comfort food spot. R'Mell lights another blunt and enjoys the music with the hot summer sun glowing on her caramel skin. As they pull up to the restaurant, Dee parks the truck in the parking lot and notices the same black car has been following them. A black old-school

Buick parked across the street and just sat there. No one got out.

R'Mell pulls out a $100 bill and says, "Here, Dee. Get my plate and y'all one too. Leave the change in the tip jar. Don't forget my lemonade. And here, Jazz, go across the street and get us a couple of bottles to sip on."

"Boss, we got company. Across the street. Black old school Buick. They've been following us for a minute. What 'chu wanna do?" asks Dee.

"Yeah, I been watching it since we left Denker. There's a black Benz to your left, same side of the street, three cars back, parked. Business as usual, ladies. Unless these fools want some problems, let's just get our food and go", stated R'Mell. R'Mell now knows she's being followed.

"What do you need me to do?" asked Staci.

"Just sit right here wit the burners. You know what to do in case some bullshit pops off", replied R'Mell.

As Dee and Jazz got out of the truck, R'Mell placed money in the envelopes, one for each lady. She pays her most trusted and loyal fam. That's why these three are the only ones she truly knows are her ride or die bitches. Diamond wouldn't have it any other way. So, to keep them that way, she will be true to them and keep them paid. But once (if ever) she feels that loyalty is broken, a bitch is dead. Staci is beside her, guns cocked. Dee returns first with the food, then Jazz with the drinks.

"Can we eat now, boss? I'm starvin' like Marvin, asked Staci.

"Greedy ass! Hell naw. I got a few details I need to discuss. But first, hit the windows and the air, Dee," ordered R'Mell.

"Sorry, boss", proclaimed Staci.

While Staci was proclaiming her weakness for food, Dee was eyeing the black car. All while they were there, the car was there. No one got out. No movement. *I think we gone have a problem,* she thought.

R'Mell handed each of them an envelope and stated, "This is for your loyalty to me. Although we've only been girls for today, I know when a bitch is real. I also know how loyal you all are to Diamond, and I hope to receive the same respect and loyalty. I gotta plan to take us to the next level, but shit gone get deep. So, my question to each of you is, "Are you down?" Don't answer right now. I want you to think hard about it cause you know how the family gets down. I need my own crew, and I'm asking you all first before I go outside my comfort zone and recruit some other bitches. I need 1000% trust, honesty, and loyalty, and no questions when told to do whatever I ask. Think about it. I'll get your responses when I need them. Now, Dee, head home. Jazz, pour us up, and Staci now yo fat ass can eat."

All laughing, Dee heads back down Century Boulevard blasting a west coast mix and the a/c. Everyone is eatin' and sippin', enjoyin' the vibe until Dee notices a few cars behind her speeding up on her left. Old school low riders blowing their horns to make traffic move out of their way.

"Heads up! Heads up!" shouts Dee. R'Mell and the crew turn to look out the back and side windows to notice the same thing. They all put down their food and pick up burners.

Two cars speed up in the right lane and pass them by while three others are slowly passing in the left lane. With at least four cars between them and the low riders, R'Mell shouts, "Lock and load, ladies! Looks like a welcome home party. This is why I said don't bring The Lady to pick me up. This bitch too hot!"

All of a sudden, shots rang out from in front and behind them. There were several men in black hoodies with red bandannas across their faces moving toward them.

R'Mell grabs her cellphone and dials Dres's number. "What's up, baby. Where you at?" asks Dre.

"Century and Hoover with a welcome party of about eight cars, takin' heat! Get here, now!" shouted R'Mell as she hung up.

Four of the cars blocked off the intersection in all four directions. R'Mell shouted, "This is how it will be working with me, ladies!"

Staci and Jazz said, "I'm down!"

Shots firing all around them, they started to return fire.

"Get us outta here, Dee!" shouted R'Mell.

Just then, Dee attempted to avoid the blockade by making a sharp left turn, but The Lady tipped over.

Chance Is Home

*T*hey killed my son. They killed my son. That's all Diamond could say to herself, and she just stared into space, sitting in her car. She burst into tears. Dayja was in the backseat just staring out the window, sucking her thumb, holding Darren's football. Diamond gathered herself together and started the car. Heading out of the County Jail parking lot, she realized she had to get in contact with Chance. Chance was on assignment in Miami to handle that lick for Dre. He has no idea his son has been murdered, and Diamond must find him to tell him.

Chance is Dres' lieutenant and what most women would call fine as hell. He was recently paroled from Chino prison and immediately went back to hustlin'. Chance has street credit, power, and status. He is known for being a shooter and not a talker. He and Dre hustled together on the Southside of Chicago. Their mothers were prostitutes and best friends. They don't talk about them much since they became men. They spent a lot of time with Chance's grandmother, Maria, and his uncle Monroe.

Maria was a beautiful Mexican from Tijuana and loved her only grandson dearly. She had grown to love Dre as an adopted grandson, too. That's how Chance and Dre are fluent in Spanish. Maria came from a rough area in Tijuana and taught

Chance the street game. His uncle Monroe was a street hustler. He taught them how to survive in the streets and how to play women. By the time Chance was sixteen, he had street credit, money, and girls.

Chance is in Miami, so the only thing Diamond can do is call Dre.

"Hey, bro. I need to talk to Chance. Can you have him call me so I can tell him about Darren?" asked Diamond.

"Hey sis. How you holdin' up?" asked Dre.

"I've just lost my baby boy! I'm furious! And I need to speak to my husband!" cried Diamond.

"Okay, okay. I already talked to Chance, and he's on the plane as we speak. So, see, you can't talk to him right now. But he will be home soon," stated Dre.

Crying, Diamond settled down a bit to tell her brother, "I'm sorry, Dre. I'm just emotional right now. I've lost my son. My daughter is traumatized and won't speak, and my husband is not here to help me. I feel like I'm going crazy. I want to just crawl into a hole and disappear. I love you, bro. Talk to you soon. Bye."

Dre couldn't get a word in edgewise. Diamond hung up before he could say he had an emergency call from R'Mell. R'Mell comes first in his life. Dre picked up his cellphone again and said, "Stoney. Grab the crew and some heat and meet me on Century and Hoover like yesterday. R'Mell's in trouble."

"Ok. We on our way", said Stoney as he hung up the phone.

Dre sped as fast as he could. By the time he got there, the scene was crawling with cops. All he could see was The Lady tipped over on its side and yellow tape all around it. The hood used to say yellow tape means "someone got dead". He couldn't see any bodies, but there were a lot of ambulances and fire trucks there. Stoney came up behind Dre and said, "It's a lot of cops out here, boss. We should go. Can't help the queen if we in jail. We gotta go!

"That's my wife, man. My wife!", screamed Dre.

Knowing Stoney was right, Dre got back in his car. Dre sped off down Vermont to Chance's house.

Chance was to meet Dre at his quiet suburban community home. Sitting on top of Paradise Lane, Dre pulls into their tree-lined driveway. Seeing the grey Mercedes in the driveway, Diamond was already home. As Dre got out of his car, the Lincoln town car was right behind him. Chance rushed out of the car toward the house, not even seeing Dre.

"Hold up!" shouted Dre.

Chance wasn't in the mood to really talk to Dre. His heart has been broken into a thousand pieces over Darren. His only son. He feels like he wants to explode; he's so pissed. And now is not the time to be on some stupid, unimportant shit that Dre is comin' at him with.

Chance stopped on the second step up to his front door and turned to see Dre running up the driveway.

"Hey, bro. Thanks for coming. I need to get inside to be with Diamond," stated Chance with sadness in his eyes.

"I know, bro. Darren was my nephew, my blood too. I just want to tell you that we gone find the muthafuckas who did this and handle our business. I was there. I saw the car, but not their faces. I don't know who's tryin' to attack us right now, but I'm sure whoever it is was behind this hit," said Dre with tears in his eyes.

"Honestly, I need to focus on my family. We can talk about strategy tomorrow, bro. No disrespect," responded Chance with tears in his eyes.

"Alright, go be with Diamond and Dayja. I'll see you tomorrow," said Dre as he turned and walked away down the driveway.

Chance opened the door to his home and saw Diamond on the living room floor holding Darren's shirt. Diamond started ballin' once she saw Chance.

"They killed our baby! Chance they killed him!" shouted Diamond.

Chance took her in his arms and just held her as she cried. The loud crying awoke Dayja. She stood in the entryway of the living room and shouted, "Daddy! Daddy!"

Dayja is a daddy's girl. Chance and Diamond looked at Dayja and then looked at each other in awe, since she had not spoken since the murder of her little brother. Dayja ran to both her parents and hugged them. They all hugged each other.

After putting Dayja back to bed, Chance and Diamond sat in their living room and began talking. The sun started to rise. Chance scooted closer to Diamond at the end of the chaise lounge and took her hand and said, "Now tell me everything that happened, baby. Don't leave anything out. I need every detail you can remember."

Diamond told him the whole gruesome story as she recalled. Chance pasted the floor while Diamond spoke but had her repeat the shooting scene because something sounded familiar to him. After Diamond made her full testimony to him, she fell asleep crying. Chance put a blanket over her while she slept. He stood over his wife in shame. *I should have been here to protect my family*, he thought. Chance pulled out his phone and asked, "Where are you? I'm on my way."

Chance checked on Dayja and Diamond before leaving out the front door. He walked out onto the driveway and got into his classic '69 candy red Corvette. As he drove to the end of his driveway, he noticed a black low rider blocking him in. He blew his horn, and the car backed up for him to get out. Chance didn't take chances, so he put his Glock on the seat next to him. Looking into the rear-view mirror, the black car was still behind him. He made a left turn to see if the black car would follow him.

Chance rang the doorbell of Dres' house. He had been let in by the maid.

"Good morning, Chance. May I take your coat?" asked Emma. Emma had been with Dre and Diamond since they were children.

Before he could ask, "I'm in here, Chance." Dre's voice coming from the den had a baritone sound to it.

Chance walks into a large den off the kitchen.

The den was large and had a man cave vibe going on in it. There was a bar, a big screen television, a pool table, and an array of books. The furniture was dark brown leather, and the fireplace was set in black marble. Anyone could live in the den alone.

"Can I get you something, baby?" asked Emma. "No, Emma. We are fine. Thank you," stated Dre. Emma slowly closed the den doors so the men could talk in private.

Dre began, "What's the emergency, bro? I'm trying to find out what's going on with my wife right now. R'Mell was in a car accident earlier. The hospital won't tell me anything, and I'm fuckin worried as hell."

"My shit can wait. What happened?" asked Chance as he sat on the couch.

" I don't know, but I'm gonna find the fuck out!", said Dre.

"Don't worry, Dre, you know yo wife is tough. Whatever happened, you know she alright. You'll see", said Chance.

Chance stood and started pasting the floor and stated, "Well, to get your mind off that for a minute, remember a year ago we had to get rid of some trash that needed taken care of after the trial?"

"Yeah," said Dre.

"Well, while Diamond recalled what happened, I noticed some similarities in how it went down," stated Chance.

While taking a deep breath, Chance continues stating, "I gave the same fuckin' order to my goons who missed the mark. The muthafuckas laid low for a while, and since we never heard anything on the streets, we chalked it up as a L. I told them to hit the nigga's girl as she was coming home from work. They sprayed the shit out of her car. When I heard about it on the news, I knew the job was done."

Chance pauses and takes another breath before stating, "But the bitch didn't die. The police had no evidence or witnesses, so I thought it was one for the books, bro."

Both men looked each other eye to eye in anger. A stare down at its peak.

"I lost my son!", Chance said tearfully while still looking Dre in the eyes.

Dre patted Chance on his right shoulder and said, "I'm sorry, bro. I know. Sit down."

Dre pointed at the chair across from him for Chance to sit in. Chance drew a sigh of relief before taking a seat.

"Now this is a fucked-up situation, bro. Diamond can never know that we were the cause of Darren's death. She would never forgive either of us. How could this happen?" Dre said shaking his head.

"We need to make sure this never happens again. I want the goons dead that fucked up the original hit. We must take care of this ourselves," whispered Dre.

Dre went over to the bar and poured them two shots of Hennessy out of the tall glass decanter.

Chance leaned forward in his chair and stated, "No one is more determined to see these niggas dead than me, Dre. The goons that fucked-up the hit and the niggas that killed my son. I feel you, bro. This IS a job we need to do ourselves. Soon. The goons will die before the sun goes down. I'll put the word on the street to find out who the niggas are that killed my boy," whispered Chance.

"But we know who was behind the original hit, bro," said Dre.

Dre interrupted Chance 'cause he knows that it means war going up against Garcia. Dre rubbed his hands through his hair and slammed them in his lap before standing up. There can be no mistakes, so planning the next moves from here on out must be precise.

After hours of planning, they toasted to their plan, and Chance got up to leave to put the beginning of the plan into motion. Dre and Chance gave each other dap, saying, " Ride or die, baby." Chance left the cozy den and out into the cold Los Angeles night air to get home to Diamond and Dayja. Chance was up at the crack of dawn, watching the morning news. He made good on his promise to make sure the two goons who botched the original hit were never found by the time he had his morning coffee and paper.

Bzzzz. Chance's phone vibrates on the kitchen counter. He gets up from the large glass dining room table and walks over to retrieve it.

" *Call me. I'm in the hotel.*"

Chance turns and looks around to make sure no one is around. He texts back, " *See you later.*"

He places his phone in his shirt pocket and sits back at the table. He hears footsteps approaching.

Diamond enters the dining room. Her eyes are puffy, and her hair is all over her head. She sits at the other end of the table. Diamond just sits there, with her head held low, and starts to cry.

Chance immediately jumps up and goes to her. He hugs her tightly and whispers in her ear,

"Baby, how did you sleep?"

Diamond is unresponsive and stares out the window, into space.

Chance knows when she is quiet that she is contemplating something. With Diamond's history, he knows his words mean nothing.

"I'm fine, baby. Just got a lot on my mind. Just want to be alone with my own thoughts for a while. You understand, don't you?" said Diamond.

"Yeah, I understand. You gonna be alright if I step out for an hour?" asked Chance.

"Yeah, I'll be fine. Go and handle yo business", replied Diamond.

They shared another embrace. Chance kisses Diamond on the forehead and grabs his jacket, then heads for the front door.

Diamond grabs a soda out of the refrigerator and sits on the lounge chair in the kitchen. She begins to daydream about her own childhood. It was much different then how the streets are today. She and Dre had a hard childhood, but the streets loved them then.

Diamond and Dre grew up on the south side of Los Angeles. Their childhood wasn't picture perfect. They were both abused in one way or another. Their father and mother were in the streets most of the time. They were often left alone to fend for themselves.

Dre started hustlin' when he was ten years old. Diamond was his bodyguard since she was 14. The streets loved them more than their own parents.

Dre hustled for a man named Garcia, she remembers. They never met "the man". His hook-up just told him he worked for a powerful man. By the age of 13, Dre was the top feeder on Fig. He was able to provide food and clothes for himself and Diamond. Diamond was already 17 and would be 18 before she graduated. She kept Dre safe on runs and on the block. She held the heat and knew how to use it.

Diamond taught herself how to shoot in the backyard with a BB gun. She got so good that Dre bought her a 9mm off the street until she could legally buy herself one when she was old enough.

Diamond made sure they both stayed in school during the day but hustled at night. Some nights went into the next day, and they would miss school, but not often. Dre was popular in school because he sold weed to some of his friends. Everyone knew who to get it from. Even the janitor bought from Dre.

Then their whole life changed. They were sent to Chicago, and Dre met R'Mell. R'Mell was a great influence on Dre. She was pretty and smart. R'Mell made Dre study after hustlin' all day. R'Mell and Diamond helped him with homework and tests. Then one day, R'Mell asked how the drug game went down, and it was all over from there. She hustled with Dre during the day after school and into the night most nights.

One day, Dre was at school and sold to an undercover cop. They took him to jail, and R'Mell and Diamond didn't know what to do. They went to his homie, and his homie told them to go sell pussy to get him out. In other words, he wasn't gonna help them. R'Mell and Diamond combed the hood. Asking everyone they knew who was "the man" and where they could find him. No one would talk. Until they came to a corner building to take a drink of water. A whore named Peaches came out of the building, looking around, and told them to come in. As they were going into the building, Peaches pushed them in and said, "Bitches, hurry up! Y'all gone get me killed!"

Peaches started saying, "I hear y'all looking for 'the man'. He hides out in different spots every night. But his favorite spot is "Status" up on 110th. If you wanna find him, that's most likely where he'd be."

"Thanks, Peaches", said R'Mell.

The girls ran out of the building as fast as they could to 105th. "Status" was a nightclub. They scoped it out from the outside to find other exit doors just in case they have to bail from the inside. The problem was how they gonna get in; they were only 17.

"We are gonna have to get dressed up tonight and find this asshole", said Diamond.

"Yeah, Imma need to find some hoochie clothes for tonight", said R'Mell. They both started laughing, but didn't see the huge guy standing in front of them at the side door.

"May I help you, ladies, with something?, he said.

"'No, we were just walking by. Thank you," said R'Mell.

As the girls laughed, walking away, the huge guy walked back into the club.

"That muthafucka was big as hell", they both said simultaneously.

They laughed again and began on the long walk home.

Later on that night, as the girls dressed, they were amazed at how good they cleaned up. Both girls looked over 18 and knew they would pass for it. Both nervous, they stood in line to get into the club. The music was blasting and you could her the chattering and laughing of the people inside.

"Next", said the bouncer.

R'Mell and Diamond walked up to the bouncer, and he looked at them, knowing they weren't old enough. He smiled at them and said, "Go on in, ladies."

Diamond replied, "Thank you, kindly."

Once they were finally inside, they looked for a man who was in the VIP area. The club was very nice inside. There was a large dance floor with small white lights and a chandelier above it. There was also a stage where Cameo was playing while the D.J.was hypin up the crowd. They walked all around the club until they saw a man sitting alone in the VIP section. He was a Hispanic man with a woman sitting next to him. He had on a black suit and looked groomed impeccably.

"Damn, he fine. I got this, Mell," said Diamond.

R'Mell sat at the bar while Diamond went to introduce herself.

"Can I get you something from the bar, young lady?" asked the bartender.

"Yes. A Sprite. Thank you," said R'Mell.

Looking over at Diamond, R'Mell couldn't help but dance to the music and look around.

"Hello. My name is Diamond. I was just wondering if you would like some company. This is my first time coming here, and hoping you can give me some pointers", proclaimed Diamond as she began to sit down.

As he scoots closer to Diamond on the red leather sofa, "I can give YOU whatever you want, baby. What's your name? Are you new in town?

Diamond responds, "My name is Diamond. And no, I'm just new to this nightclub. What's your name?"

"I'm Miguel Garcia, and I could make you rich, baby", said Miguel.

Diamond turned to look for R'Mell 'cause she just found "the man".

Diamond was startled out of her daydream when she heard glass shattering. She grabbed her burner from under the couch cushion and ran into the kitchen to see the glass from the back door broken and a football swirling on the floor.

What a Day

Later that night, as Alexis sits in the hot bubble bath of the Hotel Windsor, Bonita gets Raymone out of his bath and ready for bed. Miguel sent Bonita to L.A. because he knows his daughter. He knows Alexis will get so caught up in finding Ray that she will neglect his grandson.

"Hello, Ray?" asked Alexis, but there was no answer on the other end of the phone. Frustrated, Alexis throws the telephone clear across the room just as Bonita is entering the bathroom.

"Aye! Watch it!" shouted Bonita.

"Ugh! Daddy won't give me Ray's contact information, and the numbers I have are wrong. But I won't give up. I know who to call..." cried Alexis. "Hand me the phone, Bonita!

"What's the magic word, Alexis?" playfully asked Bonita.

"Now!" shouted Alexis.

Raymone comes into the bathroom with his imaginary airplane, running in a circle around Bonita.

Bonita, once again, bites her tongue and hands Alexis the cellphone. One day, she will get her revenge upon Alexis, and she'll never see it coming. But for now, she must do what she is told and take this life one day at a time.

Raymone asked, "Mommy, when can I go out to play? It's boring in here."

Alexis responds, "Soon, mijo. Mommy is trying to find Daddy right now. Tell Bonita to give you a treat. Then go sit down somewhere", she mumbled under her breath.

As she dialed the phone, she could hear someone knocking on the suite door.

"Who is it, Bonita?" shouted Alexis. Raymone runs into the bathroom as she is washing her legs.

Bonita opened the door. "Is Alexis here?" asked the tall, handsome stranger. Raymone ran toward the bathroom.

"Mommy, there is a tall black man at the door asking for you. Should we let him in? He said his name is Ray."

Alexis thought she was dreaming. She was stiff for a few seconds and then suddenly shouted, "Let him in! Let him in, Bonita!

Bonita lets the tall, handsome gentleman in. Ray stood six feet four inches tall, with a caramel complexion and a goatee. He wore blue jeans, a Raiders hat, and a jacket with the latest Air Force Ones. Real thugged out. But that is what Alexis loves about Ray, his street demeanor and his charm.

"You may have a seat, sir," says Bonita as she points to the couch.

Ray was the youngest of three children. With two older sisters, Ray caught hell. Although Ray's paternal grandparents raised him, he was still close to them both. They didn't grow up together, but their bond was tough as nails. Sometimes they would see each other during the summer if Ray wasn't in detention or in jail. He spent most of his teenage years in and out of jail for drug possession.

Ray was a product of the south side of Los Angeles who later joined the Marines. Two tours in Afghanistan made him the evil-minded hustler he is today. He's known on the streets as being heartless and ruthless when it comes to his money. Growing up without a mother made him hard on the females. Although he treated the hoodrats like hoodrats, Alexis was different. She could see right through his hard exterior and melt him like wax. He loves her but never tells her. Being in the streets didn't leave him much time to be the family man he really wanted to be. Too much money in the streets for him, plus he has debts to repay. The main one he owes is to her father.

Alexis is in the bathroom trying hard as hell to put on makeup and get dressed. Everything she needs is in her suitcase in the living room.

"Fuck!" she whispers.

Alexis looks in the mirror and realizes she can't pull off "sexy" without her bag.

She cracks the door open and shouts, "Bonita! Can you hand me the pink striped bag off the couch, please?"

Ray hands Bonita the pink striped bag next to him on the couch. As Bonita opens the door to the bathroom, Ray can see Alexis sitting on the bathroom stool, wrapped in a towel, waiting for Bonita to bring her the bag.

Alexis grabs the bag and says, "Thank you."

Bonita doesn't close the bathroom door all the way, and Ray can see Alexis searching through her bag like she had lost money at the bottom of it. Alexis stands, and her towel falls to the floor. Her body is glistening in the dim light, but he can see every curve, her perky breasts, and clean-shaven bush. Ray can't tear his eyes away from the door. Staring now, he adjusts himself on the couch and makes sure Bonita and Raymone aren't looking at him look at her. She is now out of view, and he is reminiscing about the last time they were together.

They were on the roof of the Stratosphere hotel in Vegas, looking out onto the strip. The lights from the street and fireworks in the sky made the moment just perfect. That's when Alexis told him she was pregnant, and she was keeping the baby. He was fresh home from duty. All he could think of was how he was going to be able to take care of her and a kid. He needed to make some money, and he needed to make it fast. He knew what he had to do and who he needed to contact.

Raymone walks into the living room and sits down in front of Ray. He looks to see what Ray is staring at. When he notices Ray looking in the bathroom, he says, "Are you staring at my mom, mister?"

Alexis walks out of the bathroom as if she just stepped out of the beauty salon. Ray stands up.

Alexis asked, "Mijo you remember why we came to Los Angeles? To find daddy, right?

"Yes, ma'am," replies Ramon.

"Well, let me introduce you to your father. Ray," says Alexis with a little hesitation in her voice. Only because she doesn't know what's going to happen next.

With the biggest, brightest brown eyes Ray has ever seen, Raymone turned and looked up at him and said, "Are you really my daddy?"

Ray paused to look into his son's eyes and take in the moment. After all this time, he finds out he has a son. This changes the game for him now. *I got a kid, a son at that,* he thought.

This is the answer he was looking for as to whether he was done being in the street or not. And having a family is his answer and relief. An instant family. *In-house pussy and a kid, now that's what I'm talking about,* he thought to himself.

Ray looks at Alexis, who's about to cry, before answering Raymone. "Yes, I am really your daddy." Ramon jumped up off the floor and gave Ray the biggest hug he's ever gotten from a child. Ray didn't know how to respond. He hugged Raymone lightly cause he started to feel something. His heart has been cold for years, and now he feels different. This feeling is confusing, and it's making him nervous. He puts Raymone down and immediately starts looking for his keys.

"Daddy, are you ok?" asked Raymone.

"Yeah, little man, I'm alright. Just got some business I need to take care of. I'll see you soon. Take care of mommy, ok", said Ray as he made his way to the hotel room door. He thinks about it, and something made him go back and kiss Raymone on the forehead. Staring Alexis deep in her eyes, with tears in his own, he turned and walked out the door.

Raymone was silent. Alexis walked toward him, hugged him, and said, "What's wrong, mijo?" Ramon sadly replied, "Did he not like me, mommy? Did I do something wrong?"

Alexis hugged Raymone tighter cause she felt his worry. She knows Ray was in shock and didn't know how to react. However, she didn't want to make things worse, so she responded the only way she knew how.

"Oh no, mijo! Your daddy is just a busy man. He loves you. And he will be back just like he said."

"Ok, mommy. Can I go play now?" asked Raymone.

"Yes, baby, you can go play now. But only if you kiss me first," requested Alexis.

Raymone gave her a big hug and kiss, then he ran into the other room to play. Alexis sat on the couch with her hands over her face, crying. Fear is what she feels because she knows she sprung Raymone on Ray. Ray is somewhere with mixed emotions right now, and she can't be with him. She feels Raymone is alright, but a little confused. Tears of sadness and regret flood her face, but her heart is broken. She hurt two of the most important people in her life, and she has to find a way to fix it.

Alexis goes into the room where Raymone is and asks, "How about pizza!"

"Yeah!" screams Raymone.

"Ok, let mommy call and order it," she replied. Alexis orders the pizza and hangs up.

The next call she makes will be to Ray after her father's service puts her through to him. He needs to hear the whole story from her. She waits on the line, but it just rings and then goes to voicemail.

Ray gets in his 2020 Chevy Impala and slams the door in confusion. He's pissed. He's hurt. And he's scared. All negativity that he doesn't need in his life right now. A son. *What the fuck,* he thought. Suddenly, his phone rang, and it was Alexis. He just lets it ring. Ray looks out the window at the dark street and says, "I can't deal with this shit right now!" He starts his car and pulls off fast. *Ring, ring.*

Ray was waiting in the parking lot of Home Depot to meet a new supplier. Someone who could take him to the next level. He wanted more weight; something he wasn't getting at the time. Thirty minutes later, he noticed a Chevy Suburban speeding up in front of him. The truck lights flashed, so he knew who it was. He reached under his seat and pulled out his gun. He tucked it in his back and got out of the car. Ray slowly began to walk to the truck when a man in a blue suit got out of the passenger door, but stood inside the door like he was holding a gun too.

"Are you Ray', said the man.

"Yeah", said Ray cautiously.

The man made a hand gesture for him to come over to the truck. Ray got to the truck, and the man opened the rear passenger door for him. He got in and took one look at his new supplier and said, "Oh, yell naw!"

"Man, what are you doing here?" said Ray.

"I'm your new supplier. You owe me, so you are gonna repay me. If not, we're gonna have a problem. You don't need problems, I hear. I already have your money..."

"Then give me my product so I can get the fuck up outta here!" shouted Ray.

"Like I was saying, I already have your money. However, I will put that toward your debt with me. Over the years, we have grown to have a mutual dislike for each other.

That's fine. But it has nothing to do with business. And this is business, so shut the fuck up and listen."

Ray didn't like the position he was in. No one knew where he was, and this person was dangerous. He only has his one gun to their four guns. He's stuck. So he has no choice but to see this through.

"Now what's gonna happen is you work for me now. I will supply you, but you owe me."

Ray looked at the men in the car, no emotion, just straight-faced. He realized he was in no position to respond like he really wanted to.

"So, where's my product?" asked Ray.

The same man, in the blue suit, got out and opened the rear door of the truck, and pulled out a green military duffel bag. He walked around to Ray's door, opened it, and threw the bag in his lap. Ray looked at him like he wanted to kill him right then and there. He opened the bag and pulled out a brick of "something".

"What is this?" Ray asked.

"That there is a 100-proof brick of pure cocaine, my friend. The real deal. There should be six bricks in the bag. That's just to start. If you don't work with me, I'll be forced to let the others know you have declined to pay your debt. Therefore, I want my money by midnight Saturday. You have the number. Now get out."

Ray sat there in disbelief. His hands were tied. Wasn't shit he could do but get out.

"You do realize tonight is Thursday, right? How in the hell do you expect delivery on Saturday?" asked Ray.

"That's your problem. Now, for the second time, get out! If I have to tell you a third time, you'll be getting out in a body bag."

All Ray could do was get the fuck on. The passenger door opened to another man in a blue suit. Ray proceeded to get out of the truck when a second man in a blue suit punched him in the face when he wasn't paying attention. Next, punches came from everywhere. Ray dropped the duffel bag and fell to his knees. He felt kicks and stomps all over his body. The pain. He tried to cover his face with his hands, but the beating just kept coming.

"That's enough," the gentleman said from the back seat of the truck.

"Next time I give you an order, Ray, you'd better do it. Let's go."

Ray heard the door shut, the truck start, and the tires pull off. He tried to open his eyes to make sure they were gone. When he opened his eyes, they throbbed and hurt. The whole parking lot of people were staring, but not one person would help him out.

Stumbling to stand, he shouted, "What the fuck y'all lookin' at!"

Ray continued to stumble to his car with the heavy duffel bag. Once he got in, he took a breath and said, "OH, my God! I feel like I just got my ass kicked." He reached up and pulled down the mirror beyond the visor and looked at his face. "Them muthafucka's fucked up my face!", Ray shouted, hitting the dashboard of the car. He reached for his cellphone in his jacket pocket; it was cracked. Dialing the phone with blood on his hands and fingers, he was calling R'Mell. No answer. He tried again, no answer. So he tried to contact Dre. No answer. He held his ribs cause he knew they were broken. Starting up the car, the phone rang. It was Dre.

"Dre, where is R'Mell? I have to speak to you both. It's important!" shouted Dre.

"Ray, R'Mell's been in a horrible accident. I'm trailing the ambulance as we speak. I'll call you back with the details, bro. I can't talk right now!" boasted Dre as he hung up.

"Fuck!", Ray screamed as he hung up the phone. As he opened the car door, he spat. It was nothing but blood. Slamming the door closed, the phone rang. Alexis was calling again.

Not right now, he thought. Driving out of the parking lot, Ray noticed an old school black Chevy sitting in the distance. He drove past it but couldn't see inside the car because of the tinted windows. He didn't think anything of it but to admire the cleanliness of the car.

Ring, ring. Alexis is calling again. Ray let it ring. With a glance in the rear-view mirror, he noticed the black Chevy behind him.

"Is this muthafucka following me?" mumbled Ray.

Ray turned on Crenshaw from Century and accelerated on the gas. He drove to Manchester and turned right. The car was still following him. So, he picked up his cellphone and dialed Chance's number. No answer. He tried to call Jazz, no answer. *Where in the hell is everybody?*, he thought.

While still observing the black car behind him, the phone rang. It's Diamond. *Why is someone calling me from Diamond's phone*, he thought. "Hello?" Ray questioned who was on the other line.

"Hey, Ray. It's Diamond", she said.

Trying not to act shocked, Ray replied, "Hey, Diamond. Where is everybody? I'm in a jam, and I can't get a hold of anybody," cries Ray.

"Ray, calm down. I was calling to tell you that Darren was murdered today. My baby is gone! And now I can't find Chance, Dre, or R'Mell. What's going on?" asked Diamond.

"Murdered! What the fuck you mean? By who? Where? What the fuck!, screamed Ray.

"What the fuck is going on! Shit! I got this muthafuckin car on my ass! Tell Dre, R'Mell, or anybody that I need help ASAP! I'm on Avalon and 26th."

All of a sudden, Ray stomped on the brakes. So did the black car. After Ray composed himself, he felt under the seat for his gun but realized those goons had taken it after they kicked his ass. Ray was defenseless. Suddenly, the doors of the black car sprang open, and he had two sawed-off shotguns in his face.

"Get out of the car, nigga!, shouted one of the men holding the gun. Ray's thinking, *not again.*

The back window of the black car rolled down as Ray got out of his car. He was limping and holding his left ribs. Looking into the car window, he still couldn't see anyone. All he heard was a familiar voice.

"You haven't done the job I've paid you for, Ray. Why are they still alive, Ray?" questioned the voice coming through the window.

"We missed Diamond this morning. But got her son instead. R'Mell is at the hospital fighting for her life as we speak..."

"What?" asked Ray.

"Yes, we got your sister as soon as she got out of jail. We could have gotten Dre and Chance at the scene, but I want them to suffer over the loss of R'Mell. So I ask my question again, why are they still alive?", questioned the voice.

"I'm workin on it! There's only so much I can do when people are whooping my ass and following me. I got life and street issues. So, forgive me if I'm not working fast enough for you", said Ray.

Just then, he felt the cold, hard steel of the sawed-off shotgun at his temple. All he could do was freeze. He didn't breathe. He didn't even blink. His life flashed before his eyes, and he even teared up. The gunman slowly moved the gun toward his mouth. Ray fell to the ground and pleaded for his life.

"You forget who you're talkin' to, Mr. Ray. Remarks such as those will get you killed in my world. Do as you're told or next time there will be no talking", proclaimed the voice behind the window.

The window rolled up, and Ray breathed a sigh of relief. As soon as he was gonna get off his knees, he felt the gun again. This time at the back of his head.

"Aw man, not like this! Man c'mon! I'm gonna do it, I'll do it!" screamed Ray.

Bang! Bang!

What the Hell is Going On!

"Mrs. Reeves, Mrs. Reeves!" R'Mell could hear a voice saying, while feeling someone tapping her shoulder. She was thinking it was that fat asshole of a C.O. R'Mell, slowly opened her eyes. Looking around, she noticed she was in the hospital. She noticed white lights over her head, an I.V in her arm, and the smell of alcohol. Trying to move, R'Mell felt pain all over. From her head to her feet, the pain was excruciating. She turned her head to the left and saw a doctor and a nurse staring at her.

What the fuck, she thought in a daze.

"Good morning, Mrs. Reeves. I'm Dr. Lee, and this is nurse Robin. Do you know where you are?"

"Hospital", muffled R'Mell.

Her mouth was dry, so the nurse gave her a sip of water through a straw.

R'Mell was confused.

Panicking and yelling, R'Mell asked, "What the hell is going on? Why am I here? What happened to me? Where's Dee, Jazz, and Staci?"

"Mrs. Reeves, calm down! I will answer all your questions once you calm down, alright," replied Dr. Lee.

R'Mell looked at the doctor like she was gonna cuss him out. Once she saw her arm was in a cast with screws poking out of it, she decided not to. She threw her head back on the bed and took a deep breath.

Calmly, R'Mell asked, "O.k., what happened to me?"

"First, do you remember anything?" inquired Dr. Lee.

"I remember my truck turning a corner and almost running into a tree. I don't remember anything else", replied R'Mell.

"Well, you and several others were in an accident on Vermont Avenue yesterday afternoon. You suffered internal hemorrhaging, a gunshot wound to the arm, a broken arm, and a broken leg. Your arm and leg are in a cast and will need to be for at least six weeks. We couldn't manage to get the internal hemorrhaging to stop. Your uterus was severely ruptured, and an emergency hysterectomy had to be done to stop the hemorrhaging. You see, Mrs. Reeves, you will never be able to conceive children. You will need to be here, in the hospital, for a couple of weeks before I can release you. Here is the button for your pain drip. Do you have any questions for me?" asked Dr. Lee.

"So you tellin' me I can't have a son?", crying R'Mell.

"I'm afraid so, Mrs. Reeves. I'm so sorry, but the accident caused so much damage," replied Dr. Lee.

R'Mell got pissed off and just got quiet for a few seconds.

"Where is my family? Where are my friends?" whispered R'Mell in pain.

"They are in the waiting room. I'll send them in. Call on us if you need anything. Have a good night", said Dr. Lee.

Meanwhile, in the waiting room, Dre, Chance, and Diamond are pacing the floor in their own thoughts. Each one with their own level of heartbreak and anger. Ray sits and watches them closely. Wandering what their next move is. Dre stops and hits the wall with a closed fist and yells out, "What the fuck is going on. Who the hell is behind this shit! My wife, man, my wife!"

Diamond calmly chimes in, saying, "Bro, we're gonna find out. We have to put our ears to the streets. Somebody knows something. My son, R'Mell, and the crew didn't deserve this. Just calm down and let's find out how R'Mell and the girls are."

"Thank God Jazz and Dee pulled through surgery", said Chance.

"Does anyone know who to call about Staci?" asked Ray.

Everybody turned and looked at Ray like he had lost his mind. He knows Staci had been raised by R'Mell and Dre since she was 14. Staci was a homeless girl living on the streets of Chicago when R'Mell recruited her. She was wild and ghetto and only was loyal to R'Mell. Her parents were killed in a drive-by when she was 10. After that, she was sent to live with an aunt, where she then ran away to be with a boy. The boy was murdered in a drug buy by a pimp named Shady right in front of her. And since Staci was the only one who saw the murder, the police were gonna put her in juvenile detention for not snitching. Meeting R'Mell was the best thing that could have happened to her and R'Mell.

Diamond walks over to Chance and hugs him, crying. They were all close to Staci; she was family. They hug each other close as Dre looks on. He has calmed down enough to sit down and breathe. But no mistake, he's thinking of everything, but mostly of R'Mell.

Dr. Lee comes back behind the curtain and says, "Your husband is here in the waiting room. I will let him come in for awhile, ok. Let the nurses know if you need anything. I'll check in on you in the morning, Mrs. Reeves. Good night", said Dr. Lee as drew the curtain closed and left the room.

R'Mell is coming off the morphine and slowly looks at her leg. She sees her toes at the end of the cast but can't move them. Her arm is also in a cast, but it hurts to move her fingers. All she wants to see is her face. *Please don't let my face be fucked up*, she whispered. R'Mell looked for a mirror. She didn't see one, so she pressed the nurse button. The nurse came in, but so did Dre.

Dre rushed over to R'Mell's bedside. He stood close to the bed and just looked at her body in the cast.

"Baby, are you in pain? What can I do?" said Dre with tears in his eyes, kissing her gently on her forehead.

"Find the muthafuckas who did this! Where's Staci, Dee, and Jazz? I wanna see my face!" shouted R'Mell.

"First things first, Mell. Who did this?" asked Dre.

"I don't know. We were headed to get some food, and the next thing I knew, old school cars were chasing and shooting at us. We were firing back as I was trying to call you. Dee took a left on Vermont, and I remember the truck hittin' the tree", proclaimed R'Mell while trying to sit up.

"Well, we all have been through some shit today. Diamond was in a hit this morning, and nephew was killed. Then someone called her and told her that the hit was meant for her, and she better get out of town. Nephew is gone, R'Mell. He was only five. Innocent," cried Dre.

R'Mell started crying, and Dre hugged her softly.

"Where's Diamond now?" asked R'Mell.

"Out in the hall with everyone else. R'Mell, we all had some type of dealings with unknown people today. As I mentioned, Ray got beaten and robbed. Chance told me he got approached and beaten while in Miami. Also, Staci didn't make it. She suffered three shots and was dead on the scene. We have to figure out what the hell is going on," said Dre.

"They got Staci. Fuck! You gotta get me outta here. I need to help find these muthafuckas!" shouted R'Mell, crying. "Not Staci!", she screamed.

Dre had to restrain R'Mell a bit because she was trying to get out of the hospital bed. She screamed in pain as she tried to move her leg off the bed.

"Stop, R'Mell. You can't move. You're not going anywhere. You can help from this bed. So stop it," said Dre.

While helping R'Mell back onto the bed, Ray limped into the room.

"Sis, how do you feel?, asked Ray while moving in front of Dre to get to his sister.

"How the fuck you think I'm feelin'. I'm in this bed fucked up while my nephew and friend are fuckin' dead!", shouted R'Mell.

"I know, sis. I'm fucked up too. Do you know who the hell is behind this shit?" asked Ray while holding her hand.

"No, but we gone find out! Do you know who fucked you up?" inquired R'Mell.

"No. They jacked me when I got out my car. I didn't get a chance to look at their faces", lied Ray. He knew exactly who they were dealing with. He knew exactly who was attacking the family.

"Sis, are you ok!" cried Diamond as she ran into the room. Diamond went to the other side of the bed and hugged

R'Mell. R'Mell started crying again when she saw Diamond. The thought of her nephew being gone because of something they may have done hurts her to her core. None of them deserves what's going on, but now they have no choice but to finish it.

"I'll be ok, Diamond. How are you holding up?" asked R'Mell.

Diamond stepped back, with her head down, and said, "I'm devastated. I'm hurt. Then I'm numb. I just can't believe my baby boy is gone."

"I can only imagine the pain you are going through, Diamond. I love and miss him too. You know we will find the ones that have hurt this family. We will come out on top of this. But what we all must do is go on with our daily lives first. We can't let them know that we are coming. We can't let them feel we have weakened. We all must stay strong until we know what's going on. Put your ears to the streets. Find these muthafuckas before someone else dies," explained R'Mell.

"Okay, baby. We on it. I forgot, Reese is out there waiting to talk to you, too. So we are gonna go and let her come in. I love you, baby," said Dre as he kissed her forehead to leave.

"Bye, sis. Feel better," said Ray.

"Bye, Mell. Call me if you need anything. Love you girl," said Diamond while hugging R'Mell goodbye.

They were all out of the room when the nurse came in.

"Mrs. Reeves, is there anything I can do to make you more comfortable?" asked the nurse.

"Yes, give me more pain medicine and some green Jello," said R'Mell.

The nurse came over and pressed a few buttons on her drip machine and said, "No problem. I'll be right back with that Jello."

As soon as the nurse left, R'Mell could feel the medicine start to work. She felt heavy all over and then felt high. She then lay her head back on the pillow and closed her eyes.

"R'Mell?", Reese said in a soft voice.

R'Mell turned her head and saw Reese looking down at her.

Groggy, R'Mell replied, "Hey, sis. I'm fucked up."

Laughing, Reese said, "You look fine. At least the accident didn't mess up your face. So do you remember what happened?"

R'Mell tried to sit up, but the morphine had her high as a kite. She sank back into the pillows and replied, "I do, but I'm high right now. Can we talk about this later?"

"Sure. I'll come back tomorrow. I love you, sis," said Reese.

"O.k. Love you too", whispered R'Mell as she dozed off to sleep.

Reese was disappointed she couldn't talk to R'Mell. She really needed to talk to her about something, and she was getting desperate. She goes back to the doctor next week, so she will just talk to her then. For now, she will let R'Mell rest.

There were footsteps in the dark room. R'Mell opened her eyes but didn't move. She could feel a presence behind her, tinkering with her medicine machine. She turned around and saw a tall gentleman with a syringe in his hand.

"Hold up. What the hell you doin'? Who are you?" shouted R'Mell.

"Good evening, Mrs. Reeves. I'm Adam, the anesthesia nurse. I'm here to give you some antibiotics. Let me get your nurse."

"Yes, please do. I don't know of any antibiotics that they want me to get. So go get her," stated R'Mell.

Adam left the room. R'Mell sat up as much as she could to wait for her nurse. Ten minutes went by, and no nurse. So she clicked the call button one more time. A half hour later, nurse Lisa came in.

"Good evening, Mrs. Reeves. Are you okay? Is there something I can do for you?" said nurse Lisa as she checked R'Mell's bandages and medicine machine.

"Yeah, there was a man in here saying he was here to give me some antibiotics in my line. Where is he? I'd rather have you in here when he does it so there's a witness," demanded R'Mell.

"Huh, no one is coming to give you any antibiotics. Let me check your chart," said nurse Lisa.

"He said his name was Adam and he was the anesthesia nurse. Check in the hallway. He was supposed to come and get you," said R'Mell."

"Well, I don't see any order for antibiotics, nor do I know of any anesthesia nurses here on staff. Are you sure he said he was a nurse?" asked nurse Lisa.

"Yes! I'm sure. He had a badge and everything. Are you telling me that muthafucka don't exist! He had a syringe! He was gonna inject me with somethin', and nobody knows who he is!" shouted R'Mell.

R'Mell's heart and blood pressure machine started beeping like crazy. Nurse Lisa called the code, and all of a sudden, nurses and a doctor came out of nowhere. R'Mell was out cold.

Code blue, code blue! Room 12! was heard throughout the floor.

"Clamps!" one doctor shouted.

The nurse put some clear gel on the clamps and handed them to the doctor.

"Clear!" he shouted once again.

Teamwork Makes the Dream Work

As the yacht sits motionless on the dock in Long Beach harbor, the Garcia family gathers around the round table in the main room. Mrs. and Mr. Garcia, their twin daughter and son, and Ray. The family is here to set a plan in motion on how they are gonna take down Dre and R'Mell. Their initial plan is already working. Now they need to come up with the final take-down.

"Does anyone know how R'Mell is recovering?" asked Miguel, looking at Ray.

"She was released yesterday with a nurse to her house for daily rehab. Dre has the house surrounded with security", said Ray.

"Ok, so their home. Just the place we need them to be while WE run the streets. Ray, I want you to continue the family and street surveillance. You still owe this family a debt, and until that's paid, you are one of us," stated Miguel with a stern voice.

Ray covered his face with his hands and then shook his head in agreement while cutting his eyes at Alexis.

"Alexis, I want you and your brother to keep working at the law firm. While your mother and I have a plan of our own", continued Miguel while kissing his wife's hand.

"Agreed?" asked Miguel.

They all said "agreed" in unity, knowing they had no other choice.

"Now let's have some fun and enjoy the scenery", stated Miguel.

No one moved until Miguel and Maria moved. Then everyone went their separate ways. Ray went out to the back of the boat and sat alone. He knows what Miguel told him to do, but then there is still family loyalty. Where is he going to draw the line? How is he going to maintain his loyalty to his family and not do what he owes? If R'Mell ever found out the secret Miguel has about him, she would never speak to him again.

As Ray sits alone, pondering what to do next, here comes Alexis to ruin his mood.

Ray knows she's coming with some bullshit, so he turns toward the ocean scenery to ignore her.

"What are you so in deep thought about, Ray. Is it me? Is it us?" she asked as she sat down next to him with a laugh.

Ray was annoyed by her questioning and sat up on the chaise lounge to move over, so he wasn't so close to her.

Ray replied, "No. I'm not thinking of you or us. My thoughts are my thoughts, ok."

Alexis stared at him and rolled her eyes in disgust, got up, and walked away. As she was hauling ass to get away from Ray, she flew by Miguel walking in Ray's direction. She knows it is all her fault that Ray is even involved in any of this. All because she wanted what she couldn't have.

Now what does he want, thought Ray.

Miguel stood in front of Ray with a glass of Scotch in his hand, while Ray was still seated. Ray looked up at his disgruntled face with humility.

"I assume you are not feeling our plans of action toward your family. Just remember that you owe me a debt. I'm quite sure you wouldn't want your sister to find out what went down five years ago. And certainly not what happened to your nephew. They'd probably kill you on the spot. Now you must make a choice. Have your family ruin and kill you, or upset me, and I kill you. The choice is yours," stated Miguel as he turned his back to Ray and slowly walked away.

Ray sat forward with his face in his hands and almost started to cry. He couldn't believe what he'd gotten himself into. The choice is difficult for him because of his family. They haven't always dealt with him, only when they wanted, but he knows they love and trust him. On the other hand, Miguel has him by the balls. Either way he chooses, he could end up dead. Ray whispers to himself, "What am I going to do. My family or these muthafuckas. I have to come up with a plan, so I don't end up dead or my people hating me. Either way, Miguel has to go down.

Six weeks went by, and no one had seen Dre or

R'Mell at the house or in the streets. Anyone who comes to the house is told to leave and call instead. They call, and no one answers. The only one allowed in is the nurse.

Staci was cremated because she had no "family" but R'Mell and the onset of the COVID-19 virus. No one could have a regular funeral in a church, so R'Mell just had a quiet prayer at the house and kept the urn. She placed it in the china cabinet next to her best friend, Monica. Monica died in a car accident back in 2006 in Atlanta. She was a passenger in the car her boyfriend was driving. They were both drunk and smoking weed when there was another drunk driver on the wrong side of the highway. That driver hit them head-on and left the scene on foot. The car he was driving was stolen. Police reports called it a hit-and-run. Monica was dead at the scene, and her boyfriend lived for three days, then passed on. So R'Mell kept Monica's ashes in memory to get justice for her death, no matter how long it took.

R'Mell stood in front of the china cabinet crying. She couldn't believe that both her best friends were gone. All she has left of them are ashes and memories. Neither of them left anything to show they were ever here. No home, no children. At least a dog. Wiping her tears, she admitted being grateful for her life. She walks away from the china cabinet to sit on the couch when the doorbell rings.

"No one should be at my damn door", she said.

Walking up to the door, she could hear Reese's voice say, "It's Reese, Mell. Open the door. We have to talk."

"Ugh!! What the hell we need to talk about this damn early in the mornin', Reese? I got other shit on my mind. What is it now?" yelled R'Mell, opening the door. Reese closed the door. They both walked toward the couch and sat down. Reese faced R'Mell and said, "I just left the D.A.'s office. They have a witness who swears she saw you leaving Mr. Layton's apartment the day of his murder."

R'Mell just stared at Reese, thinking. *What fuckin' witness?*

Snapping out of her thoughts, R'Mell asked, "Who's the witness, Reese?"

"Now you know I can't fuckin' tell you that. But if you so happen to read my file as I go to the bathroom, I won't breach my ethics", whispered Reese in R'Mell's ear.

Reese got up and walked down the hall to the bathroom. She was feeling nauseous again. She thought maybe she just had to shit, but that wasn't the case. Sitting on the toilet, Reese decided to just tell R'Mell she's pregnant. Not really knowing how R'Mell will react, she gone do it anyway. She has to tell someone and maybe the news will cheer R'Mell up.

R'Mell grabbed Reese's briefcase and placed it on the couch. Opening it, she saw several brown case files. She searched through them and came across State vs. R'Mell

Reeves. She opened the file and flipped to the tab labeled "Witnesses".

"Of course they have Jay bitch ass as the first witness!" whispered R'Mell.

Flipping through more of the papers, R'Mell came to a sheet that read "Sophia Blackmon".

With doubt on her face, R'Mell whispered to herself, "Who the fuck is Sophia Blackmon?" She thought to herself and then said," Oh, that bitch in red as Beauty's house. I got that bitch in my sights". She put the files away because she heard the toilet flush in the bathroom.

Reese then appeared from nowhere and said, "There's something I need to tell you..." as she held her stomach.

"Are you ok?" asked R'Mell. Sensing something ain't right, R'Mell sat up on the couch with concern in her eyes.

"What is it?" asked R'Mell.

"I'm pregnant! I'm scared, and I'm in love with the father but he's married", exclaimed Reese.

All R'Mell could do was bow her head and breathe. She was in shock. She was mad as hell. But there was nothing she could do about Reese's situation. Right now, her sister needed her, and she would just have to fake not being upset with her.

"R'Mell, say sumthin'!", shouted Reese.

Slowly lifting her head, R'Mell began to speak, "I'm just in shock that you're pregnant. I never thought yo ass would give me a niece or nephew. I'm really happy for you, Reese. But I have a favor to ask. Please don't mention this to Diamond or Chance yet. They are still grieving." Shifting herself on the couch, she asks, "Now, who is the father?"

"He's my boss at the law firm. His name is Alex Garcia, and he's happy too. We are gonna raise the baby together. He was supposed to tell his wife, but I don't think that's gonna happen. However, I am ok, and I hope I will have your support on this", said Reese to R'Mell as she sat down next to her on the couch.

"Of course, I will support you! But 'chu know I need to meet this boss of yours. I must confess, you are in a tough situation and dealin' with somebody else's husband..." R'Mell takes a sip of her wine. "This ain't gone be easy for you, but whatever you decide to do, I'll be right here to support 'chu", said R'Mell.

Reese smiled and hugged R'Mell. With tears in her eyes, Reese began to gather her files and place them back in her briefcase.

"I won't say anything to Diamond and Chance. They have enough to deal with right now. Although I know they would be happy for me, it's just not the time. When I start showing will be better, huh?" asked Reese.

"Reese, get 'cho ass outta here so I can get dressed to get outta here myself", shouted R'Mell as she walked Reese to the door.

" I love you, sis. No matter what, always know that". For about five seconds, neither of them spoke; they just stared at each other in the eyes. "I know, Reese. I love you too, sis. And once again, I'm happy for you", said R'Mell. Reese grabbed the door handle and opened the door into the cold, rainy morning. "Bye", said Reese. "Bye", said R'Mell as she closed the door in agony. Her heart felt like it was gonna bust out of her chest. Breathing heavily, all she could think was *My dream was taken away from me to ever have a baby.* She sat back on the couch and grabbed her glass of wine, then the phone rang. "Damn, now what?" R'Mell shouted.

"Boss, lady. Sorry to disturb you", cried Jazz.

"First of all, Good morning, Jazz. Secondly, what is it?", asked R'Mell.

"We got a problem", said Jazz.

"Girl, spit it the fuck out!" shouted R'Mell.

"There's a new eyewitness who claims they saw YOU coming out of Beauty's apartment the night he died", said Jazz. "And that's not all, I've been driving by your house and noticed one of them old school cars sittin' down the block. It's been there for two hours now".

Mell B

R'Mell sat quietly, eyes focused on the fireplace. She took a sip of wine, placed the glass back on the coffee table, and stated, "Handle the fool in the car. I'll deal wit this witness myself. Give me a couple hours to get ready and call me back."

After hanging up with Jazz and hearing Reese's news, R'Mell had had enough already, and it was only 10 a.m. She wondered *what the hell else was going to go wrong today.*

While sitting at her vanity, she kept thinking about Reese. It came to her attention that her boss's name was Alex Garcia. Could it be Miguel Garcia's son? she thought. There are a lot of people with the last name Garcia. *With everything that has happened and that's going on, could it be him,* she thought. Taking off her bonnet and brushing her hair, she stopped. "Maybe it's just a coincidence", R'Mell said to herself. "But my fuckin' gut tells me different!", she shouted. Immediately, she called Dre.

The phone rang twice and Dre said, "Good morning, baby!"

With a smile on her face, R'Mell says, "Good morning, baby. There's something I need to talk to you about. Can you come home, or can we meet for lunch?"

Dre replied, "I can be there in 20 minutes, baby. On my way."

Twenty minutes later, the front door opens, and Dre appears. R'Mell is sitting on the couch, thinking.

"I'm here, baby. What's wrong?, asked Dre as he sat down beside R'Mell with concern in his eyes.

"Reese came to see me today and dropped some fucked up news on me", said R'Mell.

"What is it?' asked Dre.

"She's pregnant. But get this, by her boss. His name is Alex Garcia. Does that name ring a bell to you?" asked R'Mell.

Dre stood up and started pacing the living room floor. Then stopped, mid-stride, and said, "Are you sure she said Alex Garcia, Mell." Confused, Dre sat back down and looked R'Mell in the eyes and continued, "If so, that would explain all the crazy shit that has been goin' on. Wait, let's not jump to any conclusions. We have to be sure. Garcia is a popular name, Mell."

R'Mell replied, "I was thinking the same things. So what I am going to do is pop up at her office today and invite them out to dinner. That way, I can get a look at this muthafucka and know if it's Miguel's son or not. We can't take any changes that it's not. We've come too far now to start slippin', Dre. Can you make dinner tonight?'

"Hell, yeah. I wouldn't miss it", shouted Dre while jumping up off the couch. "Mell, what if it is him? He knows who we are and who Reese is to us. We'd be putting her and her unborn child's life in jeopardy. Reese knows of Garcia but never knew of the twins. That's how he got to her. Miguel knows we are here then. And if that's the case, we all in danger."

Dre could feel his blood start to boil with anticipation. This was not good news at all, especially if it's dealing with Garcia. They left Chicago to get away from the life and start over, not to get pulled back in. Not wanting to upset R'Mell any further, he went to hug her, but she shrugged him off.

"What the fuck, Mell?" stated Dre.

"I have thought of all that shit too. But we have to play this cool until we know for sure. Once I invite them out for dinner tonight, I will call you and let you know if it's him or not. So answer your phone and sit on this. If it is this muthafucka, we need to call a meeting asap", said R'Mell as she then stood to hug and kiss Dre goodbye.

Now that Dre was gone, R'Mell could think. All she could think of was the bad times they had when working for Garcia. H*e found us!* she thought. R'Mell shook herself out of the trance she found herself going into. She had to get out of her head to think straight. But this was no ordinary problem. This man is not dealing with a full deck, and they must be careful about how they handle this. She poured another glass of wine and sat staring at the fireplace. Contemplating.

What felt like hours went by, and R'Mell had a plan. Looking for her cell phone, she decided to call Reese.

"May I speak with attorney Reeves, please. It's personal. Thank you," stated R'Mell.

"Transferring you now", replied Reese's secretary, Candice.

"Attorney Reeves", said Reese as she answered the phone.

"Hey, Reese. It's me. I was wondering if you and Alex were free for dinner tonight. Dre and I would love to meet him", said R'Mell.

"I am so happy you want to meet him, sis. Sure, we can make dinner. How does 9 o'clock sound at the Bel Air Hotel?" asked Reese.

"Sounds perfect! See you then", said R'Mell.

"See you then", said Reese as she hung up the phone.

R'Mell immediately called Dre. "It's all set. Nine o'clock at the Bel Air Motel. So be home by seven so I can run my plan by you first, and so you can change. Love you, bye", said R'Mell to Dre as she hung up the phone.

Across town, Chance was knocking on a hotel door that belonged to Alexis. He came to tell her that they can't talk to each other anymore. A part of him hated the attraction he had for Alexis, but he couldn't help it. The door opened, and Alexis was wearing a red-laced teddy with thigh-high boots. *Damn*, he thought to himself. She wasn't going to make this easy.

With a smile on her face that was from ear to ear, Alexis says, "Come in. I've been expecting you."

Upon entering and closing the door behind him, Chance says, "Thank you. We need to talk, Alexis. We can't do this anymore; it's not right. I'm happily married."

Before Chance could finish what he was saying, Alexis bum rushed him and kissed him. Chance embraced her and kissed her back. Their attraction to each other was more than they could overcome. Still kissing, Chance unbuckled his pants and then grabbed Alexis. He picked her up and backed her up against the bedroom wall. Alexis screamed in anticipation and held on for dear life. With Alexis' legs dangling behind him, Chance entered Alexis slowly and moaned loudly.

"Damn, you feel so good. Mmm", moaned Chance as he fucked Alexis against the wall. He then grabbed her again and threw her on the bed while taking off his clothes.

"Come and get this papi," whispers Alexis as she backs up to the headboard and opens her legs.

Chance placed his whole face in Alexis's pussy while she moaned with her eyes closed. Soon she climaxed, and Chance placed soft kisses from her thighs up to her lips. They passionately kissed as Chance entered Alexis's pussy with hard thrusts; Alexis moaned. Chance grabs her by the hips and fucked her until he climaxes. He got off Alexis and lay next to her in silence.

Alexis says, "And you were saying?"

Chance replied, "What are you talking about?'

"When you came in the door, you were saying something about us not talking anymore cause you're happily married. Do you still feel that way?" asked Alexis.

Chance started feeling guilty and began getting dressed. Chance replied, "Yes. I do still feel that way. This was wrong, and I can't do this to my family."

Aggravated, Alexis sits up and replies, "Oh, so you can fuck me but not have anything else to do with me, huh? O.k., if that's how you want it."

Alexis grabs her robe and leads Chance to the front door. Chance follows behind her, stating, "This was a mistake, Alexis. Nothing more, nothing less. So, please don't call me anymore."

"You'll be back. I ain't worried about it. You liked it," stated Alexis as she opened the door.

Startled, they were both in shock when in front of them stood Diamond. With tears in her eyes, she says, "I've been calling you for over an hour, so I tracked your phone here. Now I know why you had to leave so early this morning. Why Chance, why?"

Alexis reached out her hand and said with a smirk on her face, "Hi, Diamond. I'm Alexis. Sorry to hear about your loss. Please accept my condolences."

Diamond wanted the gun she pulled out from behind her to leave a gash in her head as hard as she hit Alexis. Once Alexis fell to the floor and begged for her life, Diamond stated, "Bitch, fuck you and your sympathy! Come for what's mine again, and I won't hesitate to put a bullet between your eyes next time!" Diamond stared at her and then turned and stared into Chance's eyes.

Chance didn't move or say anything. He didn't know what to say or do. He was busted. He knows he hurt her in the worst time of her life, and there's nothing that he could say or do to change that. Diamond walked out of the room and into the hallway; Chance followed her. Turning swiftly, Diamond pointed the gun at Chance and said, "Don't! You might as well stay cause you will never share a bed with me again!"

All Chance could do was look at Diamond standing still and let her go. He knew he was wrong, and if he moved, she'd kill them both.

Holding up his hands, he cried, "Ok, ok, Diamond. I'm sorry!"

That pissed her off. Diamond pressed the .45 hard upon his forehead and cocked it and whispered, " Fuck you, Chance". She cried and turned and walked away. All they could do was watch her and finally breathe.

Alexis says, "Stay with me, Chance. I'll take care of you. My family can protect you."

"Bitch, did you hear what I said! Don't call me anymore! I just lost my wife! Just leave me alone, Alexis!" shouted Chance as he ran after Diamond.

Bleeding and embarrassed, Alexis stepped back into the room and grabbed the first aid kit to patch herself up. Once she was finished, she grabbed her phone and said, "We have a problem. He left before I could get it, but I will get him back here somehow."

No More Lies

Diamond was driving well over the speed limit, attempting to get far away from Chance. With tears running down her face, all she could do was ask herself "why". Why would Chance cheat on her while she is still in mourning for their son? "That muthafucka!", she screamed while hitting the steering wheel. In silence, she mourned her son and now her marriage. No more tears. Only revenge is in her heart now. "They gone pay for this. All of them!"

As Diamond drove up to her house, she noticed a van parked in her driveway. It's not a good time. *Who could this be?,* she thought. "What the hell now?" she says aloud. Parking her SUV, the side door of the van opened up, and Dre jumped out.

"What's going on, Dre? Everything ok?" asked Diamond.

"Where's Chance? We may have a problem, sis", asked Dre.

"He's not here and won't be coming back", replied Diamond as she started walking toward the front door.

"Fuck you mean, sis? Where's he at?" asked Dre, grabbing her arm.

"It's a long story I don't want to relive. Did you try his cell? He'd probably answer now", stated Diamond.

"I don't have time for this shit. I got a problem!" shouts Dre as he paces the ground, attempting to call Chance again. No answer. "Fuck! Tell him to call me. It's important!"

"Is there something I can help with? I got a sitter, so I'm done. I can explain on the way, bro. Wassup?", stated Diamond as she got into the van.

"What the fuck is going on?" asked Dre while getting in behind her.

After telling Dre what went down with Chance, Diamond got pissed all over again. Only this time, no tears.

"You shittin' me, Diamond. I'm so sorry, sis. What the hell is he doing? You sure this bitch said her name is Alexis? Did she say a last name? This shit is too coincidental", said Dre as he shook his head in disbelief.

"Yeah, bro. She said Alexis. She didn't give a last name, and I wasn't trying to hear one. What's coincidental about it?" asked Diamond.

"Remember the man R'Mell, and I said we used to work for? Well, we aren't sure, but we think he may have found us. Reese is pregnant with her boss's child, whose name is Alex Garcia. Miguel has a set of twins named Alex and Alexis Garcia. We think Alex is his son, and if you came across Alexis, then we have a big problem. R'Mell and I are supposed to have dinner with Reese and Alex in a couple of hours, and I wanted Chance to put a couple of goons in the restaurant just in case', stated Dre.

"You need me to set someone in the restaurant? I won't let y'all go in there blind. Garcia probably knows all of us by now, so I can send a couple and some goons. What time are you going and where?" asked Diamond.

Dre gave her all the info and tried Chance again. Still no answer. Diamond finished her phone call and said, "They'll be there. I'll be in the area of the hotel too, just in case."

"Ok, sis. Thanks. I need to get home and get ready. Call you in a minute", replied Dre as Diamond got out of the van.

Dre makes it home and up to their bedroom. "Is that you, Dre?" hollered R'Mell from the bathroom.

"Yeah, I'm here. You won't guess what happened today. Chance..." R'Mell returned, "I already know. Diamond called. I feel so sorry for her, but she's strong. I'm surprised she didn't kill 'em both. Have you heard from Chance yet?", asked R'Mell as she came out of the shower into the bedroom.

Dre had his back turned to R'Mell as he was taking off his clothes. As he turned around to answer R'Mell, he looked at her and paused in his tracks. He stared at R'Mell as she dried off. Dre got aroused. Walking toward R'Mell with lust in his eyes, he answered, "No, and that's not like him to not check in wit me."

Looking at his wife and realizing how beautiful and sexy she is, all he could do was smile to himself. With his arms stretched out to her and a smile on his face, Dre says, "Baby, let us take a moment to relax before we go to dinner. Take a shower with me."

R'Mell turned around to look Dre in his eyes and smile. She took his face in her hands and kissed Dre. Slowly, he took off her towel, grabbed her by her ass, and lifted her up onto him. While kissing passionately, Dre walked into the shower and put R'Mell up against the glass door of the shower stall. Still kissing R'Mell, Dre used his right hand to turn on the shower. As the hot water trickled down their bodies, R'Mell and Dre were bound together in an exotic trance. Steam engulfed the air, and they devoured each other. R'Mell's legs were wrapped around Dres' body while he held her up and pushed his dick deeper with every stroke. Water beaded off his face as he watched his dick move in and out. R'Mell's moans got louder the deeper Dre entered her. After a few minutes, Dre let R'Mell down and positioned her on all fours and entered her from behind. R'Mell screamed with passion as Dre continued to stroke her deep and slow. Soon, they both let out loud moans at the same time to signal their climax. As Dre pulled out, R'Mell fell to the shower floor. Trying to catch their breath, they could hear one of their cellphones ringing. Laughing, they both started running into their bedroom.

"It's mine!" said Dre. R'Mell plopped on the bed in relief and stared at Dre to see who was on the phone.

"Hello", said Dre as he kissed R'Mell.

"Bro, we got a problem", cried Chance.

"Yeah, nigga, I've been callin' you. Where you been?" asked Dre.

"Listen, I got into some shit and...", shouted Chance.

"Nigga, I know all about what you did to my sister muthafucka!! That shit gone get dealt wit, but right now, we got a bigger fish to fry. Be here in 30 minutes!" shouted Dre as he hung up the phone.

Shaking his head, Dre stated, "That nigga lucky Diamond loves his ass, or he'd be dead right now. Plus, I need him and his peeps to secure the restaurant tonight. I ain't takin' no chances that we dealin' wit Garcia. We will know once we see him. If that is the case, we must play it cool for Reese's sake and her baby. But if that muthafucka make one small move, he's done fo'. Feel me?"

R'Mell stated, "Say less, baby. We gotta play this smooth and quiet. This nigga knows who we are but has no clue we know who he is. So, for the sake of my sister, we feel this nigga out until we leave. I already got the girls on Reese, and they will be on the outside of the restaurant the whole time we inside. Don't worry, baby, we covered."

As Dre and R'Mell were getting dressed, R'Mell's cell phone rang. It was Reese. She put her on speaker phone.

"Hey sis, y'all on your way?, asked Reese.

"Hey sis. We puttin' the final touches on our outfits. We'll be leaving in about 10 minutes. Why, you there already? asked R'Mell.

Reese responded, "No, I am waiting on the car to pick me up. I am so excited for you both to meet Alex.

Dre and R'Mell look at each other as Reese continues.

"He has been talking about meeting you all day. I hope you like him. Well, see you in a few minutes, says Reese with excitement in her voice.

"Okay, sis. See you in a few," replied R'Mell and hung up.

"If this muthafucka is Alex Garcia, then Garcia knows we here, and it's about to get serious real fast. Everything that has happened since we got here makes sense now. It's the only explanation. That Plan A we discussed before we left Chi is officially in effect, Dre. Garcia came to play, but he doesn't realize who he playin wit," stated R'Mell with a calm smile on her face.

"If it is him, I will excuse myself and let Chance and Diamond know Plan A is in effect. Once I return, you excuse yourself and take Reese with you. That way I can see if the nigga changes his attitude with y'all gone from the table. I'll give you the signal if I think we need to change our attitude and excuse ourselves from dinner, ok." said Dre.

"Got it. Now let's go", said R'Mell.

Both dressed in Gucci, they turn on the security system and leave the house. As they are getting into the Lady, cops swarm their driveway, ten squads deep. Cops get out: guns drawn.

"What the hell is going on?" shouts Dre to Detective Simmons, who's walking toward them.

"Good evening. Hello again. We are looking for Chance Steward. Do you know where I can find him? asked Simmons.

"Fuck no! He don't live here! Why are y'all here? Y'all scarin' my wife!" shouts Dre.

"I doubt that she fears anything. Your friend Chance was seen on hotel video surveillance coming out of a room where a woman was assaulted tonight. I just need to talk to him. Here's my card. Have him call me before I find him", said Simmons as he turned and walked away.

"Ok, boys. He's not here. Let's go! shouted Detective Simmons.

Dre tore up his card and threw the pieces to the ground. He watched Simmons get in his car and turned to get into the back seat of the Lady. Unaware, Chance was also in the backseat alongside R'Mell.

"Nigga! What the fuck!! We don't have time for this shit, Chance!" shouted Dre.

"Bro, how was I supposed to know that muthafucka was comin'? asked Chance.

Taking a deep breath, Dre responded in a monotone voice and said, "We have more important shit to deal wit right now. But this will get dealt wit as soon as we done wit this shit that has the potential to fuck us all. So, get yo head in the muthafuckin' game!!

Dre stares Chance in the eyes and yells, "Drive, Eddie!"

R'Mell stares out the window, thinking about every scenario this evening could bring. As long as her sister is safe, that's all that matters now.

The parking lot was empty at Fleming's, the restaurant outside of the Bel Air Hotel. Only a handful of cars were in the parking lot. Dre and R'Mell stared at each other, knowing what the other was thinking. As Eddie was pulling into a spot, R'Mell's phone rang. "Mell, where you at? Are you running late? I'm at the restaurant, and I'm the only one here."

R'Mell replied, "I'm on my way in. You ok?"

"Just wandering where everyone was", responded Reese,

"So, Alex isn't there either? Is he coming?" asked R'Mell,

"He said he's 20 minutes out. He's on his way", replied Reese.

"Ok, on my way in. See you in a minute", said R'Mell and hung up the phone.

"This muthafucka ain't even here yet. Let's go in before his ass gets here so we can see his ass comin'", stated R'Mell.

"That's cool. Everyone else is in place, and we got stashes in the restaurant already in case we need 'em. Y'all remember the plan?" asked Dre.

R'Mell and Chance replied, "Ashe'"

All three got out of the truck and walked toward the entrance of the restaurant. It was too quiet, which unnerved R'Mell. She just kept feeling somethin' ain't right. A woman only gets that particular gut feeling when there's bullshit in the mist. They can tell when they man cheatin', when somethin' is off or about to happen, or when something wrong with a loved one. Women have what's called "women's intuition," and it's seldom wrong. R'Mell scanned the parking lot and memorized where each car was and the outside of the building. As she walked through the doors of the restaurant, the hair on the back of her neck stood up. She stopped and looked around. The restaurant was empty.

Dre whispered to R'Mell, "Don't worry, I got chu. Keep walking."

Just when they entered the restaurant foyer, a beautiful, well-dressed woman appeared and asked, "Party for Reeves?"

R'Mell smiled and answered, "Yes, but why aren't there any other patrons this evening?"

The well-dressed woman said, "Our restaurant has been closed for your private party this evening. Please, follow me."

Dre and Chance gave each other the side eye while R'Mell shook her head and responded, "I understand. After you."

R'Mell turned and nodded to Dre. As they walked toward the back of the restaurant, they saw Reese waving them down.

"Just ahead is your table. A hostess will be there shortly to take your beverage request", said the well-dressed woman as she walked away.

"I'm so glad you all could make it. Thanks for coming", stated Reese.

Chance sat on the aisle seat facing the door while Dre and R'Mell sat in the middle seats facing Reese. Chance was checking out all exits and blind spots, which made him change to the next seat to his left, leaving the aisle seat open. Dre looked at Chance with concern, but he let it go to pay more attention to the women. He knew it was for a reason.

"So, where's your baby daddy?" R'Mell asked while smiling at Dre.

"Can't wait to meet him", said Dre.

"He just called before you came in. His driver was pulling in the parking lot, so he should be in shortly", Reese responded happily.

Reaching her hand out to R'Mell, Reese said, "Please be nice, Mell. I know you're gonna like him once you meet him. Dre, keep her straight, please."

After they all shared a fake laugh, they heard the front door open. They were focused on the door until a tall, dark Hispanic man walked in with two other Hispanic men. All were in suits and speaking to the well-dressed woman. As she started to guide them toward them, Dre whispered, "That's him, that's Garcia's son. Heads up."

As they approached, Dre and Chance stood, while R'Mell was sitting there trying hard not to show the hatred she had for Garcia. She was literally battling with herself, in her head, not to put a bullet right between his eyes. She could feel her blood boiling, but she had to think of Reese. So, she calmed herself, closed her eyes, and thought "boujie bitch activate".

"Alex, so nice to finally meet you", said R'Mell in her professional voice while extending her hand.

Reese, Dre, and Chance looked at R'Mell with concern on their faces cause they couldn't tell what she was on. Dre grabbed her leg under the table, and Chance changed his position in his chair. Reese stood up, grabbing Alex's arm, side eyeing R'Mell, and said, "Hi Alex. I'd like to introduce you to my family."

Tapping Reese's hand, Alex put on a fake ass smile and said, "Finally nice to meet you all. I feel like I already know you." Reaching out his hand to R'Mell and Dre, they shook hands. Only because they are there to support Reese. That is the only reason he's breathing right now. Dre stares at the other suits Alex brought with him. They stand like statues but watch his every move.

As everyone sits down, eye contact never breaks. The tension in the room is this as hell, and Reese doesn't have a clue. Dre asks, "So Alex, Reese tells us you own the law firm she works with. Are you also a lawyer?

Alex replied with a smirk, "Yes, in fact, I am. I own the firm. Reese is doing an excellent job, and I soon wish to make her a partner."

Reese looks surprised. R'Mell says in a monotoned voice, "Sis, you never told us that."

Exited, Reese responded, "I just found out as you did!"

Dre looked at Alex with a blank stare. He ain't feelin his bullshit but cannot show how pissed off he is for Reese's sake. Dre knows Alex is on some bullshit. Now they are gonna have to keep Reese safe cause he knows Alex just told him, in so many words, *I know who you are, and I'm gonna take her down with all of you.*

Dre then asked, "What is your firm's specialty. Criminal law, taxes...?"

"At Garcia and Associates, we specialize in Criminal Law. Eighty percent of our case load is drugs and guns. Reese oversees a majority of our drug cases. She has to get involved with some very nasty people. You should remind her that there are some bad people out there," replied Alex with a sinister smile.

Alex is staring at R'Mell and Dre with boiling hatred in his eyes, and they stare back at him like, *make a move muthafucka.* As they kick each other under the table, Alex just proved their theory. Miguel Garcia has been behind it, and he's coming for revenge.

R'Mell breaks her stare by spilling her glass of wine down her white Gucci dress. Sarcastically saying, "Excuse me, y'all, I need to get this out." She stands, wiping her dress, and gives a look to Reese.

"Excuse me too, baby, gonna go powder my nose. Be right back."

Dre stands and says to R'Mell with a kiss, "Don't take too long."

R'Mell let Reese walk ahead of her into the restroom. She was looking to get into the second stall. Once they entered the restroom, someone was already in the second stall.

"Pregnant sisters first, go ahead," motioned R'Mell. Reese ran into the stall, laughing cause she knew what R'Mell was getting ready to do. Banging on the second stall door, she could hear that whoever was there was not alone.

"Get out the fuckin stall and get a room, muthafucka!" shouted R'Mell. Reese was in the first stall, laughing. Then the second stall opened and out came the host and one of Alex's men, fixing their clothes. As soon as the two love birds were out of the bathroom, R'Mell ran into stall two before Reese finished her business. Talkin' shit to cover up the fact that she was lifting the toilet tank to get the Glock placed in there by Jazz earlier today. She put the Glock in her purse. Hearing Reese flush in the next stall, R'Mell poured some water from the bottled water she had in her purse into the toilet. Reese was still laughing, R'Mell flushed and exited the stall. Both meeting at the sink to wash their hands, R'Mell felt this was the opportunity to say something to Reese about Alex.

Looking at each other through the bathroom mirror, R'Mell says, "Sis, what I'm about to say to you, you're not gonna like. But I gotta keep it a hundred wit 'chu. Alex gives me a bad feeling. I mean, I know that's your baby daddy and shit, but I just don't want to see you get hurt. He is your boss," she continued. Reese looked hurt and bowed her head, then responded, "Sis, you just need to get to know him. Alex is very caring and supportive of my career and of me. Although I haven't told him I'm pregnant yet, I know he'll be happy. We're in love, Mell. I'm finally happy, and I hoped you'd be happy for me."

"I am happy for you, Reese. Are you gonna tell him at dinner tonight?" asked R'Mell.

"Yeah, I plan to. You'll see how happy he will be. Watch and see," said Reese.

Now facing each other, R'Mell holds her sisters' hands and says, "We love you and just want you to be careful wit this man. Promise me, if some weird shit starts happening, you'll tell me."

Smiling, Reese replied, "I promise, Mell. I love you too." Both women hugged and left the bathroom.

Arriving back at the table, Dre stood and said, "I was getting ready to come in there after y'all. What were y'all doing in there, shit'n?"

Alex then stood and asked Reese, "Everything ok?"

Reese replied, "We're fine. I have an announcement to make." She turns to Alex and grabs his hands. Alex looks confused and puts on a fake smile.

"Okay, this should be interesting. What's the announcement, Reese?" asks Alex while turning in his seat.

Looking in Alex's eyes and smiling, Reese says, "I'm pregnant, Alex."

Alex turned three shades of white. He couldn't even speak. All he could think of was how mad Miguel was gonna be. How does this change the family plan? This was not in the plan; *what does he do?* Is she really? Did her family put her up to this? He's in shock; he can't move.

Alex puts on a fake happy smile on his face and says, "Reese, are you sure? This is great! I'm gonna be a father!"

Chance whispers in Dre's ear that a car has been parked up the street and has been sitting for the past half hour. Dre gives him a nod, and Chance excuses himself from the table. R'Mell peeped the move, diverted the situation, and shouted, "I'm gonna be an auntie again? I can't wait to spoil my next queen! Or king! Congratulations to both of you!" R'Mell looked at Alex, who returned a smirk and shook his head to say thank you. Knowing this news wasn't what he expected.

Reese asked, "Alex, I really want this to work. Are you willing to help me raise this child?"

Alex leaned in and kissed Reese and replied, "Yes, I am. I wouldn't miss raising our child and blending our families for the world."

R'Mell and Dre had had enough of his bullshit. They were there to support Reese, but the bullshit Alex is on is enraging them, and it's starting to show.

"I'm happy. Now, we can eat. I'm starving," said Alex.

185

Everyone orders their food, and then Chance returns to the table but stands and asks to speak to Dre. "It was an old school black Buick. Ain't that the car Mell said was following her when she crashed? I started walking up the street, towards the car, but he pulled off; no plates." Dre whispered, "Put a BOLO for that car and call two more cars with burners, I don't trust this muthafucka." Chance replied, "One," and walked out of the restaurant.

Dre returned to the table, staring at R'Mell to cue her in on what's going down.

Alex asks, "Everything okay?"

"Oh yeah, our driver left and caught a flat, so we are just waiting for our backup driver and car. He should arrive in time to pick us up," answered Dre.

"If not, my driver could drive you all home," stated Alex.

I bet he would; hell naw, thought Dre.' "Thank you for the offer. But only friends and family know where we live," replied Dre sarcastically with a smile.

"Okay, no problem. It wouldn't be a problem to take you back out to Riverside. No trouble at all," Alex says just as sarcastically.

R'Mell reached into her purse to pull out the Glock, but Dre stopped her from under the table. Dre looked at her and told her to chill; he got this. R'Mell was mad as fuck; pissed! She was ready to pop his ass right at the dinner table, giving no fucks about how it would hurt Reese. This muthafucka done went too far. *This muthafucka knows we live in Riverside: he knows where, too!*

The table was quiet once the food arrived. No one said anything. Reese wondered what was going on. She felt that no one liked Alex. *Wait, how does he know they stay in Riverside? I never told him that,* she thought.

"Well, it's been an eventful evening. I want to thank my family for coming. This meant a lot to me. Thank you," said Reese while blowing everyone kisses.

Chance gave Dre a nod from the entrance.

Dre states, "You're welcome, sis. Once again, congratulations. I just got word our car is here."

Pulling out R'Mell's chair, Dre continues, "Thank you, Alex, for having us. Thank you for your hospitality. I hope that we meet again soon."

Reese replied, "WE will have to do this again, maybe dinner at my house. Thank you all for coming. Mell, let me walk you out."

As the guys stood up from their chairs, giving each other the side eye, Dre and Chance shook Alex's hand. Reese grabbed R'Mell's arm and began walking toward the entrance with Alex on their heels. Dre and Chance are right on his heels.

Reese and R'Mell hugged and kissed each other for at least a minute at the entrance door.

"You ladies act like this is goodbye. You'll see each other again real soon," Alex said sarcastically with another smirk on his face. R'Mell slowly turned her head with death in her eyes, looking at Alex.

As R'Mell opened her mouth to cuss his ass out, Dre stood in between her and Reese, grabbing R'Mell's arm and pulling her. R'Mell never took her eyes off her mark as she was being escorted out by Dre and Chance.

Dre smiled, saying with nervousness in his voice, "Yeah, ladies, it's late. Let's pick this up real soon. Good night."

Reese stood there with a look of confusion on her face. "What's wrong with your sister? Did I say something to offend her?" asks Alex with a fake look of concern on his face.

"I don't know. She has been through a tough time lately. Maybe it was too soon for this. I'll call her tomorrow. Thank you for this. I really appreciate you taking the time. Now, let's go", responded Reese. Deep down, she knows R'Mell wouldn't have responded like that for no reason. She's always been able to read R'Mell, but this was different, and she feels something is wrong, especially after her words about Alex when they were alone. As Reese and Alex walk toward their car, Reese looks back at her family standing in the parking lot staring back at her. The look on their faces lets her know, for certain, something is wrong. So, she nods to them as if to say *I got your message* and got in the car.

As Reese's car drove off, Dre focused his eyes on R'Mell and shouted, "Mell, what the fuck were you thinkin'? That shit could have gone bad as fuck, and you would have had Reese in the way! Alex knows who we are! We can't have any fuck ups while this nigga breathin'! He got Reese, bro!"

As pissed off as R'Mell already was, she had to think this time before she spoke. Dres' right. Alex has Reese. She has to be calm to think this through. She sighs and calmly replies, "First off, what 'chu not gone do is think you checkin me. Second, you right. We can't afford to make any mistakes until we have a plan. Let's go." Dre and Chance agree. Dre opens the door for R'Mell and says, "I love you, Mell". R'Mell smiles and gets in the car.

A silent ride for both Reese and R'Mell as they make their way home in two different directions. Both with racing thoughts of plans of escape in their minds. Both on the same page, hoping the other is too.

Chance's phone rang. It's Diamond. "We need to fuckin' talk. Now!" states Diamond. "On my way," replies Chance as he hangs up. As Chance looks over at Dre and R'Mell, he knows shit just got real. Still dealing with the death of his son and psychotic ass Alexis, he wonders what Diamond is gonna add to his living hell now. He needs to get his head in the game and get ready to deal wit the storm heading their way.

Dre sits and thinks of their next moves. He internally knows they're all in danger now, but he's more worried about Reese cause she's unaware of the danger she's in. R'Mell is pissed and has a mindset of killing the whole family, but knows she has to save her sister first. He needs a ruthless but foolproof plan dealing with the Garcias. They are an Opp that needs to be dealt with legally or on the streets. Either way, Dre knows the odds are against him, but he has to protect his family at any cost. He and R'Mell have come too far together to let this muthafucka win. Miguel Garcia is going down. Dre knows he has to make this happen or they'll all be dead.

That Damn Brother of Mine

Alexis sees Ray in a restaurant, sitting at the window. Although he has a hoodie on, she knows it's him cause she saw him from the street before he went in. She grabs her gun from the glove compartment and decides to wait for him to come out. Alexis stares at Ray with fire in her eyes and rage in her heart. Her feelings make it easy for her to carry out her assignment to kill him. All of a sudden, a black Escalade pulls up and blocks her view of Ray in the window. Since she no longer has eyes on her target, she decides to get out of her car to get a better look. As she gets out of her car, the Escalade pulls off, and she no longer sees Ray sitting in the window. Running across the street into the restaurant, she almost got hit by two cars. Running through the front door, she alarms the patrons in the restaurant who are all staring at her. She started running and looking all over the restaurant, but found no sign of Ray.

"Where did the man sitting in the window go, she shouted within the restaurant.

The hostess replied, "Who, ma'am? Who are you looking for?"

Alexis, confused, shouted "Shit!" Alexis turned and ran out of the restaurant onto the street. As she looked up and down the street, she pulled out her cellphone and dialed.

"I lost him! He got away! shouting into the phone. As she hung up her cellphone, she began walking across the street to get into her car. Suddenly, a truck with bright lights was coming toward her, speeding. She ran and got in to get her car started, but it wouldn't start. Four men in dark clothes jumped out of the truck and ambushed her car. They opened her door and roughly pulled her out.

Before she knew it, she was hit with the butt of a gun and passed out. Two of the men picked her up and threw her in the back seat of the truck.

Sitting the Escalade down the street, watching everything, R'Mell turned to Ray and said, "You were right, bro, Garcias are after us all", stated R'Mell.

Ray replied, "They plan to take you all out, one by one. Garcia gave me an ultimatum to either lure you to a property or he will expose my secret and kill me."

"What secret?" asked R'Mell.

"Don't worry about that. What are you gonna do? Help me figure this shit out, sis. He's out for revenge, and he wants all y'all dead. What's the plan?" Ray replied with concern in his voice.

R'Mell sat in silence for a minute, thinking she should have just popped her ass as soon as she was headin' back to her car. She was now deep in thought about a plan. R'Mell came out of her evil trance and dialed Dre on her cellphone.

"Hey, we got a problem. Call a meeting. We are officially in code black, so we need everyone there. I'm on my way", stated R'Mell. As she hung up the phone, she gave the signal to drive off.

The car holding Alexis drove behind them. As she stared out the window with the rain hitting the glass, all she could think about was how she thought their new life was gonna be. This is not the life they ran to. This is becoming the life they ran from. Inside, R'Mell is pissed, sad but not vengeful. First, the bullshit with Beauty, then her nephew, now Garcia. Now she has to put back on the mask and the attitude of her old life. Again. Being R'Mell was that part of her she grew to despise because street life was never her. She had to become her to survive. Now bullshit has presented itself again, and her family is being threatened. R'Mell is getting heated all over again, thinking about the Garcias and the shit they're trying to pull. As she says goodbye to the life she knows she deserves, R'Mell has now become a force that only sees red for the Garcia family. A thirst that only death can quench.

The foyer is dark and silent. All anyone in the dining room could hear was R'Mell's stilettos hitting the floor, getting closer. As she entered the room, everyone could tell by the look on her face that her demeanor had changed. The look in her eyes were of pure anger with tears that would not fall. *She's back.*

R'Mell started speaking in a shaky voice that demanded attention.

Gazing over the dining room to make sure all family members were present, she began saying, "We are officially in code black. Miguel Garcia and his family are the target. Personally, he has already set me up, tried to kill me, and murdered my nephew. Many of you have had something happen to you out of the blue. You now know why. You will get your marks from me individually. I want no mistakes, just results. Remember Code Black and Code Butterfly. Hit me if wit any snags. I have his daughter, so he's coming. Be ready and stand on all ten. Ashe", stated R'Mell.

Everyone got up from where they were sitting, gave R'Mell a nod, and left. She stood in front of the fireplace staring into the open flames so hard her eyes began to water. Just thinking. She had to be careful of what she said 'cause she still didn't know whose side Ray was on. Yeah, Alexis is out of his way, which he needed anyway, so it doesn't affect his mission at all. She would hate to have to kill her brother, but for the safety of her family and future happiness, she will in a heartbeat and won't give two fucks.

R'Mell was so deep in thought that she didn't hear Dre come up behind her to hug her. She grabbed his arm and swung him over her shoulder onto the floor. Then pointed the Glock at him that she had in her pocket.

"You need to chill, Mell. It's only me," Dre said jokingly.

Standing to hold R'Mell's hands, Dre continues, "I saw the change in your face when you entered the room. I see the mask is back on, which means all business. You know I'm with you, forever. We gotta do whatever it takes to finally get away from this muthafucka. Whatever you plannin' behind those eyes, I need to hear it. Blink two times, breathe, and look around."

R'Mell, staring in Dres' eyes, began looking around the room.

Dre says, "You are home. I'm with you. You're safe."

R'Mell hugs Dre and whispers in his ear, "Dubai."

Dre looked R'Mell deep in the eye for a few seconds, then kissed her passionately.

R'Mell and Dre have a plan that if they ever get separated or have to part ways for any reason, they have a meet-up spot. It was up to R'Mell to say where. They always knew that the day might come when they'd have to split up if the heat was too bad. With everything that has happened thus far, they both know that the time has come.

As R'Mell and Dre hold each other tight, they both feel like it's the last time they'll ever see each other. Like a final goodbye. R'Mell starts to cry, and Dre wipes away her tears and says, "Wipe yo eye, my little black butterfly. The woman I fell in love with, deep inside, is the one crying out right now. But my queen is a force. I really need her right now. So, channel her and let's get this business handled."

With tears in her eyes, R'Mell looked at Dre and replied, "Baby, I know we handle business with the utmost tact and detail, but I got a bad feeling somethin' gone go wrong. I know I've been off lately, but this feelin' is comin' from my gut. I've been feelin' weird, but I know I'm right. All I ask is for you to be careful and do our hourly check-ins. Dre, I love you so much. Our life was supposed to be better than this. That's why we came here in the first place: to have a better life than what we left behind. Now we back to where we left off, but in a worse fuckin' predicament. I feel we've been cheated of happiness. I just want to grow old with you and watch the sunset every night, with you."

Dre wiped the tears running down R'Mell's face as she was seemingly growing angrier. He stepped back as she squatted to her knees in silence. Dre knew not to try to console her right now; just let her compose herself by herself. She will be fine. It's like watching a Transformer from the movies take another shape. When she does this, he knows his queen will eventually emerge.

As R'Mell slowly rose, she straightened her dress, exhaled, and said, "I'm good. Let's show the Garcias shit ain't sweet."

Dre smiled and replied, "There she is! My caterpillar has come out of her cocoon. Let's fly, my Black Butterfly, let's fly."

Dre took R'Mell's hand and led her upstairs to their bedroom. They fucked all night to the early mornin'. Then slept in each other's arms until the maid knocked on the door at noon. They both got up and into the shower, where the fucked for an hour before the maid came back. Both now dressed: R'Mell in Chanel and Dre in YSL. They approved each other's fits, then Dre's cellphone rang.

"Who dis?" asked Dre.

"Hey, bro, it's Ray. I got a construction deal for you. This nigga named Jay wants to renovate a condo over on Sunset. Can you come over and check it out?"

"What is he looking to do and how much he is talkin' first?" asked Dre with interest.

"Shit, he wants it gutted and then remodeled. It's two floors with a decked roof. It does have a crack in the foundation, but I told him you can handle that. He says money no object," replied Ray.

"Who is this nigga?!" asked Dre.

Ray stated, "He one of my military guy's brothers; he a street nigga. He solid."

"Yeah, his ass better be. We ain't got no time for any more bullshit right now. Aight, text me the address. I'm on my way," replied Dre and hung up his cell.

"Dre, Ray is my brother, but I still don't trust his ass. Watch yo back. I don't want to have to kill my brother, but I will", stated R'Mell.

"Calm down, you know I got this. I'll be a'ight. Just gonna go clock this money and back to the business at hand," smiled Dre. He kissed R'Mell goodbye while walking out of the bedroom. R'Mell slumped down on the bed and lowered her head because this was the warning Ray gave her last night in the truck.

It's finally sunny outside, but evil is in the air. R'Mell sits at her desk finishing up with her soldiers' assignments toward her plan. She makes sure her plan is tight down to the slightest detail. Ruthless and efficient. Timed. She drinks from her glass of wine when her cell rings.

Mom, R'Mell says to herself, looking at the caller ID.

"Mom?" answers R'Mell as she stands at her feet. Her mother never calls her. She takes care of her parents in silence. They don't speak because of circumstances during their childhood, but she still takes care of them both, nonetheless.

"Mell, we both love you, honey", says R'Shawn, her mother.

Before R'Mell could say anything, a familiar voice came chiming in like a voice from a horror movie.

"I need proof of life," said Miguel Garcia.

As R'Mell started walking toward the basement, she replied, "One moment."

R'Mell opened the basement door and proceeded to walk down the stairs with stiletto heels, crashing each step. Reaching the bottom of the stairs, her soldiers nodded. There, with both arms spread out, was her enemy's daughter. She walked up to Alexis, slapped her awake, then put the phone up to her face so Miguel could hear her.

"Speak, bitch!" shouts R'Mell.

"Daddy, come get me!" screamed Alexis as the call ended.

R'Mell paced the basement floor for about an hour, slapping and punching Alexis every time she passed her, waiting for her cell to ring. Two hours passed, and her cell rang. It was one of her soldiers who was assigned to her parents' house. She slowly answered the phone. All she heard was, "Sorry, boss. We were too late."

R'Mell replied, "Complete 2nd phase of your assignments and get back here," as she hung up the phone. R'Mell squatted to her knees in rage and pain. The soldiers assigned to Alexis looked at each other but were told by Dre to never assist or touch her when she is mad.

"Boss Lady, do you need help?" asked one of the soldiers.

R'Mell raised her arm and held up one finger in an effort to say she's good, give her a minute. The soldier stepped back a little and gave a concerned look to the other soldier. After another couple of minutes, R'Mell slowly rose with tears in her eyes. The two soldiers had a scared look on their faces cause they've never seen R'Mell this way. So, they both paced themselves cause they didn't know what she was gonna do. She walked over to soldier number two, grabbed his AK-47 from his hands, and pointed it at Alexis.

Alexis started screaming, "No! Please don't! I have a son! He's your nephew!"

R'Mell froze for a second and thought to herself, *That damn Ray.* Could she look her nephew in the eyes knowing she killed his mother?

"Hmm, if what you say is true, I'll take care of him. Too bad he'll never get to meet his grandparents because of yo' bitch ass daddy. So, tell the devil I said wassup, bitch!"

R'Mell emptied the entire clip in Alexis, dropped the gun to the floor, then spit on Alexis as she turned to the shocked soldiers standing in front of her.

"Drop this bitch on Miguel's yacht and leave my mark on her ass!" said R'Mell.

"Yes, Boss Lady," said soldier number one in a trembling voice.

R'Mell pulled out her cell as she was walking back up the basement stairs to call Diamond.

"Diamond, Phase 2, you're up. Go get Reese now and bring her here," R'Mell said in a soft voice.

"R'Mell, I'm sorry, and I got chu," replied Diamond softly as the call ended.

R'Mell then dialed Dre. No, answer. *He must still be with that new client*, she thought.

"That's what it better be, for Ray's sake", R'Mell whispered to herself.

Am I My Sista's Keeper

As Diamond hung up the phone, with a look of concern on her face, Chance asked, "What's wrong, Diamond?"

All she could say, softly, was "Phase 2." Diamond looked at Chance and continued, "What we have going on has to be put on the back burner for now. Please remember your passport and identification. I have an assignment just like you, so I have to go. We'll finish this later."

"For whatever it's worth, Diamond. I am. Truly sorry," said Chance.

"I know. You should be. Now look at what happened. I hope she was worth it," said Diamond as she walked out the door and slammed it shut.

All Chance could do was stand there looking stupid. He had to get his head in the game and finalize his assignment. He pulled his cell phone from his coat pocket and dialed Dres' number. Voicemail. Dre always answers his phone. So, he called R'Mell.

"Dres' not answering his phone. Is he with you?" asked Chance.

"No, I've been trying him for the last hour. He left a few hours ago to meet up with Ray and a new client. That's all I overheard. With Ray in the middle of this, something is off.

Ray's phone goes to voicemail, too. I got my girl getting a ping on Dre and Ray's phone. Just waiting for a call back. When she calls back, I'll hit you wit the address," replied R'Mell.

"Bet," replied Chance as the call ended.

Driving along LaBrea Avenue, Diamond checked in with her crew to make sure her assignment was tight and ready to roll. Everyone was in position and waiting for their cue. She texts them all and says, "Go." Next, Diamond called Reese.

Reese was sitting in her office, doing paperwork. The office was made of all glass walls and doors, so no one had any privacy to scratch their ass if they needed to. Although she had her own office, it was still very noisy since the receptionist's desk was right outside her office door. Writing her notes for court, she suddenly heard her personal cell phone ring. It was Diamond. If Diamond is calling her, it can't be good.

"Reese, this Diamond. Don't say a word, just listen. Say, "This is she". I know your office is bugged, so do as I say. Now say, "Hello, Mr. Blackmon, how may I help you?"

Reese said exactly what Diamond told her to say while looking around the office.

"A woman is getting off the elevator. She is gonna ask the receptionist to speak to you. Her name is Sophia Blackmon. Say, "Ok, when did all this occur, and is she a witness to this murder?" Reese complied. Diamond continued, "Stay on the phone with me until the receptionist comes in and says you have a visitor. Meet Ms. Blackmon at the receptionist's desk. Follow her lead. I'll be waiting. Now say, "Ok, Mr. Blackmon, I think I can help you. I will transfer you to my receptionist, and she'll schedule an appointment for you to come in and talk to me. And then end the call and follow her", said Diamond as she ended the call.

As soon as Diamond hung up, the receptionist came in to announce she had a visitor. Reese repeated what Diamond said, stood up from behind her desk, ended the call, and walked out to the receptionist desk to greet Mrs. Blackmon.

"Hello, I'm Attorney Johnson. How may I help?" said Reese.

Reese had never seen this woman before, but she understood the assignment Diamond just gave her. With recording devices and cameras all over the office, she had to do as she was told.

"Hello, Attorney Johnson. My name is Sophia Blackmon, and I have some information on one of your cases you are working on. I got your name from the Public Defender's office, and I really need to speak to you", said the woman.

"Ok, come right in my office, and you can tell me more about it," said Reese as she motioned to the woman the way to her office.

The receptionist was listening and staring while the phone was ringing.

Glancing at the receptionist, the woman continued, "I would prefer to speak to you in private and preferably not here. Do you have a few minutes to have lunch with me in the cafeteria?"

Reese replied, "Sure, just let me grab my purse. I'll be right with you."

Reese turned to enter her office and realized that the woman was Jazz in a wig and glasses. Which means R'Mell sent for her, and something is wrong. Grabbing her purse and coat, her office phone began to ring. She glanced down at it, and line three was ringing. It was Alex. She grabbed both her cell phones and headed for the door.

"Gail, I'll be out of the office for lunch with a new client. Be back in an hour," said Reese to the receptionist as she was getting on the elevator.

As the elevator arrived, Reese said," A..."

The woman quickly cut her off and said, "Shhh."

As they reached the lower level, the elevator doors opened, and the receptionist yelled, "Attorney Johnson, there's a call for you."

The woman said, "Keep walking and don't answer her." Once they got outside, a black Escalade was waiting. The woman said, "Run, Reese. Now!" Reese ran down the stairs as fast as she could. Then she heard, "Stop. Stop!" The building security guards were behind them.

"Hurry, Reese," yelled the woman.

Reese jumped up in the back seat and closed the door while the woman hopped in the passenger seat, and the truck took off. Reese witnessed the security guards writing down the plate number.

"Would somebody please tell me what's going on!" shouted Reese.

The woman took off her wig and glasses. It was Jazz.

"Calm down, Reese. You remember Dee? Diamond sent us to get you by way of R'Mell. We're taking you to Diamond now. She will fill you in. Just relax, we'll be there in a few minutes once we know we haven't been followed. You need water?" asked Jazz.

"No, I'm ok," said Reese calmly.

"Hit the switch, Dee. We can cut across Vermont and come back around. Diamond at the spot on Normandie anyway", said Jazz.

"Gotcha," replied Dee.

"We got company! Three cars back on your left. That black old school Buick, again. Just drive normally and put on your hat, Dee. We changed the plates so we good", said Jazz.

Suddenly, Jazz hops over the passenger seat to the back. Takes off her dress and pulls down her pants. She lifts the seat and pulls out an AK-47 and a shotgun. Pulls out a fully loaded drum and a Glock. She handed the Glock to Reese.

"You know how to use that?" asked Jazz to Reese.

"My sister ain't raise no bitch", laughed Reese and Jazz.

"Well, we may have a problem heading our way, so get ready", said Jazz.

Reese pulled off her coat and turned around to look out the back window. She saw the black Buick Jazz was referring to. It looked familiar. She had seen it at Alex's house a few weeks ago when she went to pick up some paperwork from his house. She remembers cause she parked right behind it in front of his house. *Alex has something to do with this situation*, she thought.

"Turn down 122nd, Dee. See if he follows us then," said Jazz.

Jazz then pulls out her cell and says, "We got company, Diamond. We just turned on 122nd & Vermont heading toward Normandie. Waiting to see if he follows us. Ok, Ashe."

"Dee, if he follows us to Normandie, head to the Vermont spot, and she'll come behind him and box his ass in. Then we let his ass have it," said Jazz.

"Ok, I'm a block from Normandie. Do you see him?" asked Dee.

"Naw, where'd he go?" shouted Jazz.

"I don't know. I don't see him either. I'm gonna go down to Vernon and double back to the spot just to make sure", said Dee.

"Ok, I'll let Diamond know", replied Jazz. Fifteen minutes later...

"Hey, we don't see him anymore, and we just turned onto Vernon off Normandie, headed to you..."

Just as she told Diamond where they were, a shot came from a high-caliber rifle and struck Dee in the head. Dee was gone. The truck picked up speed heading into oncoming traffic on the left side of the street. Jazz grabbed the steering wheel and got the truck on the right side of the road, but Dee's foot was stuck on the accelerator. Jazz struggled to keep the truck from hitting anything or anybody while trying to move Dee's lifeless body out of the seat. As Reese looked behind them. The black Buick was right behind them.

"He's back!", Reese shouted.

"I see him!" returned Jazz, sitting in the driver's seat, getting them closer to the spot.

"I see Diamond and Chance behind him! I hope he got an army in that car cause it's about to be a war!" shouted Reese.

Jazz's cell phone rang, and she answered it and replied, "You sure. Ok, I'm pullin' over."

Jazz pulled the truck over and hopped in the back with Reese. They both stared out the rear window to see the black

Buick at the last red light waiting to proceed. Then they saw three masked men hanging out the window of the Buick. Jazz cocked the AK and had it pointed at the rear window. All of a sudden, Reese says, "Wait. Look!" Behind them was Chance's truck that had a masked man hanging out the window with a rocket launcher. Car tires burned behind them, seeing the horror in front of them. Most turned around to go in the other direction. Cars on the opposite side of the road stopped or pulled over to watch what was about to transpire.

Laughing, Jazz says, "I'm finna video tape this shit!"

"Shouldn't we take off or something?" shouted Reese.

"Chile, this truck, in fact, all our trucks were bulletproof. You safe right here while Chance behind us. Just watch the show cause this finna be epic as fuck!" stated Jazz, excited.

The light turned green, and the black Buick must have just noticed what was behind them and tried to speed off. The men hanging out of the Buick were so focused on the Escalade that they didn't even notice Chance behind them. Once they noticed, they started firing at Chance's truck, so the man hanging out of Chance's truck released the rocket launcher. They tried to get out of the black Buick by climbing out of the windows they were hanging out of, but it was too late. The rocket went through the rear window, and the black Buick exploded into a thousand pieces in an instant.

"Damn, did you see that shit, Reese! And I got it all on video in the middle of Vermont!" shouted Reese.

"That was clean, and no innocent people got hurt", replied Reese.

"You sure you and R'Mell are sisters?" joked Jazz.

"Ok, we gotta get outta here. Hold on. Gotta get you to the spot for the drop off", shouted Jazz as she got back in the driver's seat and took off. She kept the truck running.

Ten minutes later, they pulled into an alley where Diamond and Chance stood waiting.

Reese jumped out and ran to Diamond.

"Thank you, sis. I didn't have a clue what was going on. It must be serious if it got to this point just to get me from work," said Reese.

"Are either of you hurt? Reese, you good?" asked Chance.

"We good. We lost Dee, though. R'Mell gone be mad about that", said Jazz.

"Don't worry about that, Jazz. I'll let her know. Phase 2, now Jazz." Said Diamond.

Jazz paused for a second and replied, "I'm on it, Diamond. Hope everything is ok with you, Reese. And I hope we didn't scare you. Later, Ashe"

"What does Ashe' mean?" asked Reese to Diamond.

"Never mind that for now. Reese, we have bigger problems. I need to take you to R'Mell. Let's go," said Diamond.

"So, neither of you is gonna tell me what's going on?" asked Reese.

"R'Mell will explain everything when we get there", replied Chance.

Reese got her stuff from the truck Jazz was in and put it into Diamond's truck. Once she got into the passenger seat, Diamond stated, "Please don't touch any buttons or knobs in here. None of the buttons or knobs does what you think they do. I repeat, do not touch anything up here."

"Are there special buttons or knobs in the back? asked Reese.

"Ok, well I'm gonna sit in the back cause I don't want any gun, no knife, no darts, no poison coming in my direction," laughed Reese while getting out of the passenger seat into the back of the truck.

Diamond laughed and responded, "Smart move, sis-in-law! You remembered!"

Diamond's cell phone rang. "Yeah, we on our way now. Hit a snag, but we took care of it. No, I've tried calling him too. It goes straight to voicemail. Be there in 10 minutes."

As Diamond turned up her driving music, Reese stared out the window, wondering what had happened that R'Mell had to go to these great lengths to get her out of the building, and why a man and a car affiliated with Alex were chasing them? She then reaches into her purse and grabs both her phones. She received ten missed calls from the office on both phones and five missed calls from Alex's number on her personal phone. She turned off the location on both phones and powered off her work phone.

Reese looked out the window and noticed they were approaching an airplane hangar.

"What are we doing here?" asked Reese.

"This is where everyone is. R'Mell is here' replied Diamond.

As the sky was dark, all the other hangars had lights on the top of their roofs. However, there were three hangars with no lights, and the doors were closed. Men with guns were seen walking in front of them as if they were guarding gold. There were at least 30 cars parked in front of it, including a police car, which was weird to Reese. Diamond pulled right in front of the door. Two soldiers approached Diamond's truck and opened the doors.

"Hello, Ms. Johnson. I'm here to escort you to Boss Lady", said soldier number one.

"And Ms. Diamond, I am to escort you in", said soldier number two.

Both ladies got out of the truck. Reese looks at Diamond with concern on her face, and Diamond nods and mouths to her, "It's ok".

Reese follows the soldier to the back of the hangar, where there is a black door. There is a camera above the door. They step inside, and the soldier closes and locks the door.

"Follow me," he said to Reese.

After climbing two flights of narrow stairs, they came to a long hallway with another door. Behind that door was a little room with chairs and a receptionist window made of bulletproof glass. A camera hung right above the glass window, and a keypad was next to another door.

Soldier One entered a code, and the door opened. He opened the door and let Reese inside.

R'Mell sat on a couch, staring into a fireplace with a glass of wine in her hand.

"Mell, what's going on?" said Reese.

"Reese, come sit with me, and I'll tell you everything you need to know", said R'Mell.

An hour had passed, and R'Mell got to the Alexis situation, and she had to tell Reese their parents were dead. Reese didn't say a word; she just cried. She leaned on R'Mell, and they cried together for about ten minutes. A knock on the door startled them into reality, and the door opened. It was Diamond.

"Everyone's here, R'Mell. Can I help y'all get cha selves together? "asked Diamond. "I know what you both are going through, and it's not easy. At least you have each other. By the way, R'Mell, I have more bad news. We lost Dee today, but we got the black Buick" relayed Diamond.

"Dee was family. Make sure she's given a queen's burial and pay for the funeral. We are mourning too much right now to make ANY mistakes going forward. We will be right down," replied R'Mell.

Diamond left and closed the door.

R'Mell turned to Reese and held up her pinky finger and said," Am I my sistas' keeper?"

Reese replied, "Yes, I am."

R'Mell said, "So let's get these muthafuckas!"

A Deal with the Devil

R'Mell gives everyone straight and detailed assignments. No mistakes, no excuses. As Reese stands beside her, she notices that Reese has tears rolling down her face. Losing her parents this way hit her hard, and being pregnant doesn't make it any easier. Diamond led her to sit down at the table.

"At this point, I feel and believe Miguel has Dre with the help of Ray," said R'Mell.

Reese said, "Mell, he's yo brother!"

'Let me just say this, everyone got an assignment. Everyone. So, if I ain't trippin', why should you?' asked R'Mell.

"Chance, I release you and your people cause y'all got a flight to catch. Everyone else, remember we are in the Final Phase. Code Butterfly for others. Make sure you have your passports and meet at the rendezvous port in three days. We are a family, and nothin' comes before family. Ashe," stated R'Mell.

Suddenly, the door opened, and the two soldiers who dumped Alexis appeared with someone with a sack over their head.

R'Mell shouted, "Explain this shit!"

One of the soldiers replied, "Boss Lady, we completed our assignment, but as we were leaving, a witness came out

215

screaming. So, we took the initiative to kidnap her and bring her to you."

"Why would you kidnap her and bring her here to me?" asked R'Mell.

"Cause who it is," replied the soldier as he lifted the sack.

R'Mell's eyes widened as she stood in disbelief. Were her eyes deceiving her? Mrs. Lopez? Could this actually be, Mrs. Garcia?

R'Mell walked over to the soldiers and said, "Well done. See Chance for your promotions."

Both soldiers nodded and said, "Thank you, Boss Lady". One of the soldiers found a chair and made the woman sit down in front of R'Mell.

"Well, family, this saves us some time. Now, Phase Two of the Final Phase is in play. Team Blue remains with me. Everyone else, you have your assignments. Ashe', said R'Mell.

Everyone nodded and got up to leave. Team Blue sat down, and R'Mell continued.

"With this bitch now bein' here, I need to split the assignment down the middle, minus four of you staying here to guard this bitch. Go outside and delegate, and I need two inside, two outside, Ashe", said R'Mell.

The team nodded and walked outside the door. R'Mell got up and walked around the long table, tapping her long nails against the table, to where the woman was seated in the chair. Staring her in the eyes, R'Mell bent down so they were face-to-face and said, "Mrs. Lopez? Or should I say, the real Mrs. Garcia. You gone soon be dancin' with your daughter in hell, you old, crusty ass bitch!"

Mrs. Garcia stared back at R'Mell and replied, "Right behind you and your husband, bitch!"

R'Mell stood straight up and punched her in the face. Then grabbed her by her hair, snatched her head back, and punched her in the nose.

"Fuck!" as she shook her hand in pain.

Mrs. Garcia laughed and said, "That's all you got?"

R'Mell looked as if she was crazy and had to exhale cause she wanted to kill her so bad.

Grabbing a towel off a small table, R'Mell wiped her hand and replied, "Naw bitch! That ain't all I got, but you gone soon see a taste of what I got. It's especially for you. It's a surprise. I hope you like surprises. Fuck this shit, I need one mo' just for you talkin' shit!!"

R'Mell proceeded to unleash all her anger on Mrs. Garcia's face and body until she passed out. Once R'Mell noticed she was passed out, she whispered in her ear, "Now let's see if yo bitch ass husband can recognize you now, bitch!"

R'Mell patted Mrs. Garcia on the back and proceeded to walk out of the room. Once she reached the door, the two soldiers standing there nodded to her, and one opened the door for you to leave.

R'Mell was awakened by her cell phone ringing; it was Chance.

"We finally made it. No issues. We are setting up and will be heading out within the hour. I'll call you when we're ready", said Chance.

"Ashe', replied R'Mell and ended the call.

R'Mell was feeling sick this morning. She was nauseous and sluggish.

"What did I eat yesterday?" she thought. She went to the bathroom and threw up. The bathroom was a mess when she got through. R'Mell felt like she couldn't stand, and her head was pounding. She made it to bed and passed out again.

Three hours later, R'Mell faintly heard her cell phone ringing. She reached for it and answered in a weak voice, "Yeah?"

"R'Mell, this Chance. We ready. You ok? You need help?" asked Chance.

Speaking weakly, R'Mell replied, "No, I don't feel good today. Stand down for a little while. I'm gonna go to the doctor right quick. Wait for my call."

"Do you need Diamond?" asked Chance.

"She was my next call. Like I said, wait for me," said R'Mell and ended the call.

R'Mell called Diamond next and told her what's up and get ready.

An hour later, R'Mell and Diamond were in her doctor's office. R'Mell is lying on the office patient table, and Diamond is in a chair reading a magazine. Dr. Stewart entered the room, and R'Mell told her how she was feeling. The doctor sent in a nurse to draw her blood and gave her a specimen cup to piss in.

An hour later, after R'Mell fell asleep again, the doctor re-entered the room.

"Mrs. Reeves, I have the results of your lab work. You're pregnant. About four weeks," said Dr. Stewart.

R'Mell immediately sat up and said, "I know you fuckin' lying!"

"What my very blunt sister-in-law is trying to say is, are you sure?" asked Diamond.

"It's ok, Diamond. R'Mell and I have a certain rapport; I understand her. "And yes, I'm sure," replied Dr. Stewart.

Diamond looked at R'Mell, who was in total shock. She couldn't tell her reaction due to her staring at the door and tapping her foot.

"Are you ok, R'Mell? Do you need a few minutes alone to search your feelings after hearing this news?" asked Dr. Stewart.

"Dr. Stewart, with all due respect, please don't try to psychoanalyze me right now. Could I just have a few minutes alone with my sister-in-law? Thank you," said R'Mell.

Looking at Diamond, Dr. Stewart replied, "Yes, of course."

Making sure no one was listening behind the door, Diamond closed the door.

Diamond sat next to R'Mell while she whispered, "You know this changes things. You can't be involved with the plan at this point. I'm saying what my brother would say right now. You are in the house for the next three days, understand?"

R'Mell whispered, "After my accident, the doctor told me I had a hysterectomy and would never have children. I'm so confused! I need him so much right now. I gotta get him back by any, and I mean any means necessary. We made him a father, and that's the greatest gift I could ever give him, and no one, especially Garcia's, is gonna take that from him. No one is to know, Diamond. Ok, get me outta here."

Diamond opened the door and called for Dr. Stewart to come back in.

"You ok now, R'Mell?" asked Dr. Stewart.

"I'm good," replied R'Mell while gathering her purse and getting off the table.

"Ok, I'd like to see you back for your first prenatal visit in a month. Please see the receptionist on your way out. Seen you soon and congratulations," said Dr. Stewart as she turned to leave and closed the door.

R'Mell made her appointment, and Diamond took her home.

After eating a salad and changing, R'Mell had her driver take her to the hangar. Upon getting out of the truck, one of her soldiers told her Mrs. Garcia had been complaining about needing her medication, or she would die. *Fuck is this bitch diabetic or something?* R'Mell thought.

The soldier opened the door for R'Mell to walk through. When she entered, she saw Mrs. Garcia slumped over, as if she were already dead.

"Bring me some orange juice, now!" shouted R'Mell.

A few minutes later, a soldier appeared with a bottle of orange juice and a straw. R'Mell opened the bottle and inserted the straw. She then slapped Mrs. Garcia awake so she could drink the orange juice. Mrs. Garcia drank half the bottle and said, "Thank you."

R'Mell replied, "Bitch, you ain't gone die on me before I get my husband back. Now wake up. It's almost time for your surprise."

R'Mell set up a laptop on the table in front of Mrs. Garcia. She pulled out her cell and said, "I'm ready."

On the laptop screen was an old woman with tape around her mouth and tears in her eyes. There was also an old man who looked beaten with tape around his mouth, and a woman with her head down. All strapped in chairs with a soldier standing behind them with guns.

"Surprise!" shouted R'Mell as she gave her Vanna White over the letters' hand impression.

Mrs. Garcia started screaming in Spanish and crying.

Shouting at R'Mell, "What do you want?"

R'Mell slammed the laptop shut and replied, "I want my husband. Can you make that happen?"

"I don't know, I don't know," cried Mrs. Garcia.

"Well, you better hope yo dried up ass pussy is good enough for yo husband to want back at this point or yo fam is dead," replied R'Mell.

"What do you need me to do? I'll do it," cried Mrs. Garcia.

"Good, I knew you would see it my fuckin way. All you have to do is convince Miguel to let Dre go! yelled R'Mell.

"You know he's not gonna do that knowing you have me," replied Mrs. Garcia with a smile on her face and a sarcastic voice.

"We gone see about that, bitch! Let's call him and see just how much you really worth to him", said R'Mell as she pressed buttons on her cell phone.

As she paced the floor in front of Mrs. Garcia, deep down inside R'Mell wanted to just kill this bitch and be done with it, but she had to play the plan out. This has to go as planned, or Dre is dead. Dre being used as a ploy to get to Garcia was part of the plan she hated. However, the plan has an outcome of them being rid of Garcia for good, so she had to continue to play her part. The life she and Dre wanted is so close, and she is not gonna let anything stand in front of their happiness.

R'Mell put her cell phone on speakerphone until Miguel answered and said, "You ready to make a deal?"

"What kind of deal do you think I'd want to hear?" replied Miguel.

"Don't listen to her, Miguel! Don't listen to her!" shouted Mrs. Garcia.

"Mommy! Is that you?" asked Miguel.

"Yes, pappi! Yes!" replied Mrs. Garcia.

"Enough of the family reunion shit! You gone make a deal or what?" shouted R'Mell.

Silence...

"What the fuck is it gonna be, Miguel? I want my husband! The fuck! Pussy got yo tongue or somethin'?", asked R'Mell.

"The Forum. Two a.m." Miguel hung up, and all that was heard was a dial tone.

Mrs. Garcia was silent. She stared at R'Mell as R'Mell paced the floor. She stopped in front of the fireplace to give the illusion that she was thinking or nervous. Not knowing that R'Mell and her family already have a plan in place. R'Mell was actually waiting on Mrs. Garcia to react so she knew which plan she was gonna enact until two a.m.

Suddenly, Mrs. Garcia dared to announce, laughing, "You know you're a dead bitch as soon as you make the exchange. MY HUSBAND doesn't make deals. You and your husband are as good as already dead, bitch!"

That's all R'Mell needed to hear. R'Mell turned around and stared Mrs. Garcia in the eyes and told her, "Naw, that's where yo dumb as wrong, BITCH! I got a surprise for you!"

Mrs. Garcia looked back at R'Mell, confused and with tears in her eyes. She watched R'Mell as far as she could, and then all she could hear was her stilettos walking toward the door. The door closed behind R'Mell, and Mrs. Garcia cried out like she was in pain. Speaking in Spanish, she just started yelling. Yelling so loud, the soldiers kept having to tell her to shut up. Finally, they got tired of her yelling and hit her on the back of the head with the butt of their gun. She'll sleep until two a.m.

One Man's Battle

D re was badly beaten as he was hung by his arms. Garcia's men worked him over ever since the phone call with R'Mell. Two of them took turns inflicting blow after blow, but Dre took them all. Each blow just pissed him off more to kill these muthafuckas, especially Garcia. He just stood by, watched, and laughed. But Dre was laughing too, 'cause he knew what was coming next. Garcia waved his hand, and the men stopped.

It's one a.m., and Garcia and his men are meeting in the next room while they have Ray watching over Dre.

"You ok, bro?" whispered Ray. Ray's assignment was to give Garcia the impression that he chose to continue to work with him to set up Dre and R'Mell. Bringing Dre to the warehouse, thinking it was a client interested in remodeling it, was genius, in Garcia's eyes. Once Dre got there and saw that there was no client, and Ray kept saying he was on his way, he knew Ray was lying. He turned to leave and got ambushed by Garcia's men.

Dre was playing as if he were passed out, but was listening to everything being said by Garcia. He did hear Garcia say that he needed just the two men cause Ray was going too, and he was keeping him on a short leash. They all turned to look at Ray and Dre.

225

He whispered back to Ray, "I'm good, bro. Just remember your assignment, and we all live."

Just then, Garcia and his men returned to the warehouse where Ray and Dre were.

"Get him down and put him in the car. Ray, get extra guns and meet us at the car," ordered Garcia.

Ten minutes later, two black Suburban's pulled away from the warehouse that Garcia owned and headed toward The Forum. Ray was in the car with the two men, and Garcia traveled alone. This bothered Ray a little 'cause he felt like he was also a prisoner. His assignment is working smoothly. R'Mell will finally accept that he can be trusted. As long as he does his part, the exchange should go down without a hitch.

Dre is sitting between Garcia's men, but they don't realize his hands are no longer bound. He wiggled out of the weak knot they tied as soon as he got in the truck. Although his body is badly bruised and sore as hell, it's goin' down as soon as R'Mell gives the signal. He's gonna keep the rope in his hands just for show for now. Hopefully, R'Mell can keep her cool with Garcia so the plan will work, and they'll all be free of him. But with her, you never know.

Approaching the Forum parking lot, the truck's headlights flash twice, so the truck stops. When Garcia got out of the car, his men grabbed Dre and exited the truck. Ray stood closely behind Dre.

R'Mell and two of her soldiers were standing in front of a truck with Mrs. Garcia, blindfolded, on the ground. Seeing the beatdown on Dre pissed her off; however, she had to stay in character for the plan to go down. She hated his part in this 'cause she knew he was gonna have to get hurt. But Dre is as hard as a nigga gets, and she knows he's good. Still, seeing it hurt.

R'Mell stepped forward and said, "Garcia, how you wanna play this?"

"Give me my wife, and I won't kill you," replied Garcia.

This muthafucka must not know who he talkin' too, thought Dre as he laughed to himself.

R'Mell laughed and shouted, "Since you feel like dat, we gone do it like dis!"

That was the signal. R'Mell shot Mrs. Garcia in the head, and she dropped to the ground. Her soldiers took out Garcia's men, whose guns were filled with blanks. Garcia was shooting at R'Mell, but then Dre attacked him to the ground. Dre was beating his ass until he saw headlights approaching the scene. R'Mell shouted, "Let's get the fuck gone!" They all jumped in the truck and pulled off, leaving a beaten Garcia and his two dead men behind. Something they will live to regret doing.

"I'm proud of you, Ray. You really came through for your family and proved your loyalty," said R'Mell.

"I appreciate this shit, sis, family first!" replied Ray.

R'Mell turned her full attention to Dre. Touching and inspecting his body to make sure he was alright; she was relieved he was ok.

"Are you ok, baby?" asked R'Mell.

"You know me, babe. I'm good. Are you ok?" replied Dre.

"I'm good knowing my family is good. At least that muthafucka know who he dealin' wit now. We all worked together and got this nigga and his bitch ass wife. Garcia ain't dead, and his son is out there too. They gone want some get back, so we just have to stay vigilant until we get them two. But right now, we have to meet up with the rest of the family and debrief. I'm just gonna enjoy myself for the next week on the beach and get my drank on," said R'Mell, laughing.

"Shit, me too!" shouted Ray and Dre simultaneously.

Everyone got through TSA and onboard their flight. There were stares and whispering as they boarded because of the battle they had just been in, and the bruising people noticed on Dre. They sat in their first-class seats, ate and drank, while people wondered how they got first-class seats.

"Y'all ain't never seen black people enjoying success?" shouted R'Mell as she rolled her eyes at the other first-class passengers. After celebrating their win, they all slept until they reached their final destination.

Never Saw This Comin'

Six months have passed since the Garcia fiasco, and the family has moved on with their lives. Diamond and Chance worked through their marriage and are now raising their baby girl, who loves to play in the tree house Chance finally finished building. She sits up there for hours talking to her brother in heaven and having tea parties. Jazz and Daisy moved in together and have their own business teaching self-defense classes to women and children. They have Staci's son in the classes, too. Ray works with Dre in construction, which has kept him out of trouble and closer to the family. Reese is now nine months pregnant and due in a couple of weeks. It's been a hard pregnancy for her, but the family has been very supportive. She works for the Public Defender's office now, which keeps her busy.

After finding out he was gonna be a father, Dre has been extra protective of R'Mell. Since his construction company has taken off, he's asked R'Mell to become his office manager so he can keep an eye on her. R'Mell sold her parents' real estate business and assists Dre in getting his business off the ground. They are finally where they want to be and have left that "other life" behind them.

On a rainy Sunday in June, R'Mell was lounging on the couch flipping through a magazine when her cell phone rang.

She's like not today, I just wanted to relax. She grabbed her phone and saw it was Reese, so she answered it.

"Hey sis. How you feeling?" R'Mell asked.

"Mell! Mell, my water just broke!" panicked Reese.

"Where are you?" replied R'Mell.

"At work!" shouted Reese.

"Ok, call an ambulance, and I'll meet you at the hospital," laughed R'Mell.

Three hours have passed, and the whole family is in the hospital waiting room to be there for Reese. Although Reese is still in early labor, the family has taken over the labor and delivery waiting room. The kids are playing games, and the adults are just talking amongst themselves.

Chance notices a nurse who looks familiar. He excuses himself from the conversation to go to the bathroom. He sees the nurse again talking to a doctor, but can't get close enough to make out her face. Chance just lets it go and goes back to the waiting room, but it gives him a strange feeling. He pulls out his cell phone and makes a call for two soldiers to watch Reese and her baby until they are released, just in case. With the Garcias still out there, he doesn't want the family to get caught slipping.

After another hour, "It's a boy," shouts R'Mell, coming down the hall in the scrubs she was given to be in the delivery room with Reese.

"Reese and the baby are fine. He was 8 pounds with a head full of hair. He fine, too!" smiled R'Mell.

After a couple more hours, the family had their faces pressed to the nursery window to see Reese's son. He was adorable with fat cheeks and thick, jet-black hair. The family blocked the whole window, whereas other people there to see their babies couldn't even see. A nurse came to tell them that visiting hours were over and it was time to leave. Labor and Delivery just wanted all of them to leave.

R'Mell kissed Dre goodbye and told him she'll meet him at home 'cause she wanted to stay with Reese and the baby a little longer.

"Bro, I need to talk to you about something. Can I come by in about an hour?" asked Chance.

"Yeah, bro, I'll be there," replied Dre.

After the family left, Chance pulled Diamond aside and told her about the nurse. She told him to tell Dre and R'Mell. Diamond took Dayja home. Chance went to see Reese. Reese was asleep, so he motioned to R'Mell to come into the hallway.

"Sis, earlier I thought I saw Alexis' maid here as a nurse. As a matter of fact, I'm positive it was her. So, I called for two soldiers to be here around the clock until they both go home", said Chance.

"Are you sure, bro?" asked R'Mell as she paced the floor.

"Yes," replied Chance.

"I know you haven't told Dre yet 'cause he wouldn't have left."

R'Mell paces the floor faster now, while rubbing her stomach. She knows her heart rate is up cause her own baby is flipping around.

"I didn't mean to upset you, sis, I..."

"No, this is a family issue. Go tell Dre. Tell him to call a midnight meeting. I'll be there soon," whispered R'Mell.

As R'Mell went back into the room with Reese, Chance gave strict instructions to the soldiers standing guard by her room and the nursery. He did a walk through the department to see if he could locate the nurse, but she was nowhere to be found. Chance left and did what he was instructed to do.

R'Mell grabbed her things and kissed Reese on her forehead before she left. As she was leaving, a short Mexican nurse tried to enter her room.

"May I help you?" asked R'Mell.

"Hello, I'm here to check her incisions," replied the nurse.

"She just got to her room a half hour ago. Her incisions were just checked in the recovery room. What is your name?" asked R'Mell, noticing she didn't have on a nametag or hospital badge.

"My name is Bonita. I just started today," the nurse explained.

"Well, Bonita, until you get some credentials, you will not be entering this room. Understand?" stated R'Mell.

"I'm just doing my job, ma'am," the nurse said.

With an attitude, R'Mell replied to the nurse, "You won't be working in here until we see credentials, ma'am!"

"Do not let anyone in this room who is not family until I get back," R'Mell told the soldier at Reese's room door. She also told the soldier watching the nursery that no one is to touch Reese's son until she returns. Chance was right, that is her. Bonita from the doughnut shop.

As R'Mell got into the truck, she noticed an old school Chevy parked in the parking lot with the lights on. Making a mental note of the car, she got in the truck and told her driver to keep a lookout. Greg drove off and headed toward Vermont to get on Highway 10. R'Mell looked in the rear window and saw the same car. She lowered her head and thought, *"Here we go again"*.

"Greg..." started R'Mell.

"I see 'em," replied Greg.

R'Mell reached under her seat for her Glock and dialed Dre.

"Baby, we being followed by an old school Chevy. We on the I-10 headed home..." said R'Mell.

"They are speedin' up, Mell," shouted Greg.

"Steady, Greg. Let them get closer," shouted R'Mell.

"Lead them to the house, Mell. Be careful, baby, you carrying our child. Chance and I will be waiting", shouted Dre and hung up.

Greg drove, and they followed all the way to Riverside. So, they knew they were actually being followed. Followed right into a trap.

After a certain marker on their block, R'Mell knew soldiers were waiting. As they drove closer to the house, she knew the car would be stopped and surrounded. Suddenly, shots rang out behind her. As she turned around in the back seat to get a better look, she was struck and fell backwards against the passenger seat. R'Mell knew she was hit cause her chest was in pain and she felt dizzy. She could feel the truck accelerate and then stop. She heard Dres' voice, but she couldn't speak. It was hard for her to catch her breath. She felt extremely tired and just wanted to sleep. So, she closed her eyes.

R'Mell slowly opened her eyes. Attempting to focus her eyes, she tried to speak. With cotton mouth, she shouted, "Dre!"

"I'm right here, baby. You and the baby are fine. You were shot in the shoulder, but you're gonna be okay," said Dre.

"I can't feel my arm, Dre", screamed R'Mell.

"The doctor said the numbing feeling should go away in a few days. Calm down! You're gonna raise your heart rate, and that will hurt the baby. So, calm down," explained Dre as he was stroking her face and kissing her.

With widened eyes, R'Mell asked, "Where's my sister? Reese!?"

"Mell, she's right next door. We moved her room, so I can watch over you both," replied Dre as he smiled.

"I need to see her and my nephew. Did she name him yet?" asked R'Mell.

"Yeah, she did. Let her tell you what she named him", said Dre.

"Be right back", said Dre.

R'Mell looks around the room and sees a lot of cards and flowers. She takes an inspection of her bandages and IV meds. Suddenly, Reese and her nephew enter the room.

"Bitch, bring yo pretty ass over here with my nephew!" R'Mell told Reese.

Reese walked around to the window side of R'Mell's bed and bent over and kissed her forehead. She then passed the baby to R'Mell, who actually started to cry.

"Sis, you gone have trouble keepin the bitches away with this one!" R'Mell said, laughing.

"What is his name?" asked R'Mell.

"His name is Romello James Johnson," said Reese as she smiled at R'Mell.

R'Mell held out her hand to Reese and smiled as a tear rolled down her cheek.

"Hey, Ro. I'm your auntie Mell. We got the same name," whispered R'Mell.

"Mell, I have to take him to the nursery so he can get his final check-up before we get discharged tomorrow", said Reese while picking up Romello.

R'Mell kissed her nephew's forehead and reluctantly gave him back to Reese. As Reese was walking out of the room, R'Mell blew them a kiss, see you later.

"See ya later," said Reese as she walked out of the room to the nursery.

"You're being released tomorrow, too, baby", said Dre.

"Cool. So, what happened after I was shot? asked R'Mell.

"We stopped the car, but like the last one, it was bulletproof, so the car got away. We lost three soldiers," said Dre.

"Have the soldiers been replaced?" asked R'Mell.

"Of course. We still solid," replied Dre.

"We are under attack again. Just when we all found our peace in life, this muthafucka raises his bald ass head. Call Diamond and tell her to go buy baby supplies now and bandages for me. We both checking out now. Someone go get Reese and nephew", said R'Mell.

R'Mell sat up and ripped out her IV and went to stand, but her legs gave out on her. Dre caught her before she hit the floor. She stood to get her balance while holding out her arms.

"I got it. I got it!" shouted R'Mell.

Meanwhile, Reese rushed back to the nursery to get Romello. Once she opened the door and showed her wristband to the nurse, she looked in his bassinette, but Romello wasn't there.

She looked in the incubators and still didn't see him. Panic set in.

Rushing over to the nurse sitting at the nurses' station, "Where's my baby?" shouted Reese.

"Your husband came and got him five minutes ago, Ms. Johnson", cried the nurse.

"Bitch, I'm not married!" shouted Reese.

The nurse rushed to the phone and announced, "Code Adam, Code Adam in Labor and Delivery."

Reese ran back to her room and looked for his bassinette, and it wasn't there. Dre ran out of R'Mell's room, "What's going on?" shouted Dre.

"He's gone! Someone took Romello!" shouted Reese.

"Fuck! R'Mell, we gotta get outta here, now. Garcia is here!" shouted Dre.

"Chance..." began Dre.

"I got chu", replied Chance as he and one of the soldiers ran down the hall to locate Alex or Bonita.

"Come on, baby, let's go," said Dre as he helped R'Mell into a wheelchair.

Dre made sure Reese had all her things, and he and a nurse wheeled both R'Mell and Reese out to the truck. Once he got them both in the truck, they took off. Reese cried the whole way home, and R'Mell just stared out the window.

R'Mell is heartbroken; she feels like she was caught slippin'. If she hadn't got comfortable with their new life, she would have seen this coming. Just as she finally had her whole family back together, here comes the bullshit. She will never get to put R'Mell away and just stay Mell. There is always gonna be more bullshit to deal with. When will she finally have peace? She has to end this once and for all.

After they both took a shower, R'Mell joined Reese on the living couch in front of the fireplace. She poured a glass of wine for herself and sat next to Reese, who was still crying.

Grabbing Reese's hand, R'Mell began, "Sis, I know how you feel, and you know I am gonna get nephew back. My gut tells me it was Alex, and I will kill him for this, sorry to say it that way, but I'm dead fuckin' serious. He's dead, Reese."

Reese turned to R'Mell, looked her in the eyes, and said, "Let me shoot the first shot."

R'Mell hugged Reese tight. "It's time for the meeting. I'll be back soon. Love you, sis. Get some rest. Reese just kept staring into the fire."

R'Mell wiped her sister's tears away and stood up and walked down the hall to the basement. No stilettos, but the family could hear her boots hit each stair as she came down slowly. With tears in her eyes and a tightness in her heart, she looked at her family and smiled.

"Family, the peace that we have built has once again been disrupted by the same muthafucka. Now, they have taken another part of us that is innocent. I am concealing the rage and pain I feel inside for these people for the sake of my nephew. But that same rage and pain WILL get him back..."

Ring, ring...it's an unknown caller on R'Mell's cellphone. She answers it on speaker phone.

"Who is dis?" shouted R'Mell.

"You took someone precious to me, so I took someone precious to you", said Alex.

"The difference is, I will get my nephew back. Your mommy's never coming back", said R'Mell sarcastically.

"That is true. But if you don't give us Ray, you will never see this precious child again. Now, you have a family dilemma. A man for a child. Which do you choose?" asked Alex.

"When and where for the exchange?" replied R'Mell.

"One hour. The dock," said Alex as the phone went dead.

"Okay, I need soldiers at the dock with three shooters and a boat. Everyone else set up a perimeter half a mile around the dock. Ray, in my office. Ashe, everyone," ordered R'Mell.

Ray and R'Mell went upstairs to her office while everyone else left to get set up.

"Come in and close the door, bro. Have a seat," said R'Mell.

R'Mell stood by the fireplace and stared at the fire. She hadn't a clue how to proceed with this exchange. She'd have to choose her brother over her nephew. This time, she's actually scared. She had a flashback of when Ray would keep her safe as a child, but can she guarantee his safety now? She's pregnant and can't participate like she needs to ensure his safe return. For the first time, R'Mell feels she can't keep her family safe.

Ray sat in silence. He was terrified on the inside because he knew he'd be the one to be sacrificed this time. He chose not to go against his family last time, but now he has to pay for it. Ray hopes R'Mell has a plan to save them both. He's a nervous wreck. He's starting to shake. Silently, he prays. He wants to continue his new way of life.

"Bro, this is the hardest plan I've had to figure out, and to be honest, I don't know what to expect. It's easier if I had a family member of his, but I guess we killed them all already. Wait, where's your son?" asked R'Mell.

"I haven't seen him in a while. Most of the time he's with the maid, Bonita", replied Ray.

"Where does she live?" asked R'Mell.

"Shit, I don't know, Mell. I don't get to see him. Alexis made sure of that," responded Ray.

"We pressed for time anyway. Ok, something tells me a boat is involved in this exchange. So, you go with them on his yacht. I'll have a team waiting in the water once they pull out. Just be ready, bro," said R'Mell.

"I got chu, sis," as he stood to hug R'Mell. Ray and R'Mell looked at each other as if they knew this was goodbye.

"Okay, let's go," said R'Mell.

The ride to the dock was silent, both staring out the window. The air at the dock hits you first, smelling of seaweed and iron. There was also a hint of fresh-cut lumber from a nearby yard. The scenery was full of rows of uneven cargo containers shimmering in the moonlit saltwater. Once they reached the dock, they didn't see anyone. No one. Didn't even see Garcia's yacht. *What's going on,* R'Mell thought.

Ray and R'Mell looked at each other and shrugged their shoulders. Even the seagulls overheard were silent. The distant horn of a ship moving through the harbor was a loud echo through the visible empty dock.

Ray turned toward R'Mell and said, "Mell, if I don't make it home with you tonight, know my sacrifice is for you and my nephew. I've done some shit in my life that I deserve to be here for. He wants me 'cause I betrayed them..."

R'Mell interrupted Ray with tears in her eyes to say, "And you think that is supposed to comfort me right now. You promised me as a little girl you'd never leave me out here alone. I'm not gonna let you go that easy."

"Mell, this is me protecting you and Reese. Y'all are all I have left. You're not letting me go. I'm giving you back to what matters. Sometimes loving somebody means you take the hit they shouldn't have to. I promise you will see me again. Let me do this for the family. Raise my nephews stronger than we are. Make sure they know family is worth fighting for," replied Ray.

R'Mell hugged Ray and said, "There's got to be another way. The Garcias can't win!"

R'Mell stopped talking as if she heard something around her. "Shhh, you hear that?"

Ray was very still and listened, and whispered, "I hear him!"

R'Mell and Ray both slowly opened their doors and got out of the truck. R'Mell could hear a faint baby's cry. They began to walk around the dock trying to hear where it was coming from. Since they couldn't pinpoint in what direction the sound was coming from, they split up. R'Mell stayed closer to the truck. Greg used the headlights for her to see. Ray went further back by cargo containers. The further back he went, the louder the cry got. He came upon one where the cry was the loudest. He called out for R'Mell, but she couldn't hear him. He peeked in but couldn't see anything, so he opened the door. Inside was a baby in a car seat next to a speaker.

"Mell, I found him!" shouted Ray.

"Where are you!" shouted back R'Mell. She turned and ran back by piled-high cargo containers, shouting his name. Greg jumped out of the truck with his gun and followed her.

"Ray!" she shouted again.

"Over here," replied Ray.

He ran into the middle of the container and grabbed the car seat that had Romello in it. Once he picked up the car seat, a second door appeared and started to enclose him in.

"Mell!" shouted Ray.

R'Mell and Greg found Ray, but the grinding rumble of the cargo door quickly started to close with Ray inside.

"Ray!" shouted R'Mell as she ran to the cargo container she heard him from.

Ray quickly slid the car seat out of the holder before the door closed. Once the final clank settled in place, it was pitched black inside.

"Ray! Ray!" shouted R'Mell and Greg as they tried to open the container door.

There was a rising hydraulic hiss that came from overhead. It was a crane. The crane came out of nowhere, lifted the holder in the air, and placed it on a cargo ship there on the dock. There was nothing R'Mell could do.

Dre, Chance, and Diamond came running from behind a pile of containers. R'Mell reached down and picked up her crying nephew, holding him tight against her chest.

A loud horn crackled, and then they heard, "It's over, R'Mell. I got what I want, plus a bonus. Tell your sister goodbye," claimed Alex in a calm tone.

R'Mell froze. Every muscle in her body locked up. Her breath stopped halfway in her throat.

"Mell, help me!" cried Reese.

R'Mell couldn't tell where the voices were coming from because the mist of the dock was thick as smoke.

"Reese! Where are you?" shouted R'Mell.

"Over here, R'Mell!" shouted Alex in a playful tone.

She turned slowly toward the massive cargo ship looming at the dock, its bow rising like a steel mountain. A spotlight snapped on, illuminating a figure high on the bow with their arms pulled back, and hair whipping in the wind.

Reese. Reese was wrapped in rope with a cement block attached to her feet.

R'Mell dropped to her knees. Diamond grabbed Romello from her arms and placed him in the truck. R'Mell just stared out onto the ship, in silence. No one touched her. No one spoke.

Reese.

Ray.

Her last pieces of home.

A sound escaped her. Not a scream, not a cry, but something between the two with tears falling fast and hot.

"Not her," she whispered. "Please, God, not her too."

Dre screamed out, "This ain't over, muthafucka!"

"If I see the police or another boat, I will throw her into the ocean. I won. Goodbye, R'Mell," laughed Alex.

"Mell, take care of Mello for me. Make sure he knows I love him more than life itself. Raise him. Teach him everything you taught me..."

R'Mell raised her head when she heard Reese speaking. The ship was moving. She tried to run toward the dock, but Dre and Chance held her back.

"...Raise him to be a better man than his father!"

R'Mell froze and focused on Reese's face. Her eyes were wide, a mix of fear, love, and a silent apology. The wind continued to whip her hair across her face, but R'Mell's eyes stayed locked on Reese. R'Mell knew her sister was terrified, and she couldn't save her.

"I'm coming, Reese," shouted R'Mell.

Reese's eyes followed her sister's voice as she mouthed "I love you".

As the fog thickened, the ship became a shadow, and they were gone.

"Reese! Ray!" shouted R'Mell as she stared into the dark.

As Dre approached R'Mell from behind, she sank into a squatted position, screaming. Dre motioned for everyone to stand back and give her space.

R'Mell prayed for the first time in months for forgiveness, patience, and wisdom. Most importantly, for the protection of her siblings, her family and friends, and the loved ones they've lost. As she finished her prayer, a warm and comforting peace flowed through her. And that was the moment R'Mell stopped breaking. That was the moment she evolved into something else entirely.

R'Mell raised her head. Her eyes were swollen, her face streaked with dried tears, but something new flickered behind her expression. A quiet, dangerous clarity. The kind that didn't come from rage, but from resolve. She stood slowly, her legs steady. Rubbing her baby bump and taking one last look into the darkness that stole enough from her. R'Mell exhaled, long and slow. She turned to see Dre, Diamond, Chance, and Greg staring at her with love and concern.

"All I want right now is to hold my nephew and deliver my son. The Garcias think we are broken. We will never be broken. The Garcias have finally crossed the line they can't come back from. I know we're all hurting, but we got family we can't give up on. From this point on, we move like one body, one mind, one purpose. We're getting our family back. And the Garcias, they gone learn exactly who they just declared war on." recited R'Mell.

Diamond brings R'Mell her nephew. R'Mell holds Romello tight as he sleeps. She whispers, "Auntie gone bring your mommy and uncle home if it's the last thing she ever fucking does!!"

As everyone hugs R'Mell and Romello, Greg walks back to the truck. He leans against the truck and pulls a pack of cigarettes out of his jacket pocket. As he begins to pat his cigarettes, he notices small flashes of light on top of two cargo containers. Not wanting to ruin a family moment, he realizes they may be surrounded. He lights his cigarette and walks over to Chance, smiling, offering him a cigarette.

"Nigga, you know I don't smoke," laughed Chance.

Smiling, Greg says, "We got at least two behind you on the top of the containers and one behind the truck." Chance took a cigarette and acted like he was looking for a lighter, and walked to open the rear of the truck. Greg stood in front of Dre and the ladies and repeated what he told Chance so they could move toward the truck. Still talking and walking slowly, Dre shielded R'Mell, and Greg shielded Diamond.

"Y'all keep walking to the truck and don't look back," said Dre.

As Dre and Greg remain standing face to face, talking, R'Mell and Diamond secure Romello in the truck and get in. Chance placed guns in the back seat while searching for a lighter he didn't need. They all have on vests and Diamond covered Romello's car seat with three more.

Chance lit his cigarette and closed the rear door of the truck. Diamond climbed into the driver's seat, waiting to pull out. R'Mell called her soldiers on her walkie-talkie and ordered them all to get ready.

Suddenly, two shots rang out, and then shots could be heard all around them. Dre dropped to the ground, crawling toward the truck. Chance ran over to help Dre, but caught one himself. Greg was already down with a shot to the head. Shots echoed off the steel container walls with the light of fireworks. Diamond started the truck, screaming for Chance and Dre to get in. R'Mell jumped out to help Dre get Chance in. He was shot in the back, screaming in pain.

"R'Mell get in!!" shouted Dre.

Every shot felt amplified. Car tires screeching and then one final shot. Dre was shoving Chance in the backseat while R'Mell pulled him in. Dre staggered. His body jerked once as the air punched him. His eyes widened in a way that told R'Mell everything before he even fell.

"Dre!" screamed R'Mell.

Diamond screamed, and they both jumped out of the truck. With sirens getting closer, they knew they had to hurry. R'Mell held Dre tight as Diamond grabbed his feet. Just then, two soldiers came and finished lifting Dre into the rear of the truck. They made sure R'Mell and Diamond were inside, safely, and hopped in and sped off.

"Stay with me, Dre", R'Mell whispered, her voice cracking. "Please stay with me."

Diamond was rocking back and forth, holding Chance tight. She was telling him to hold on and shouting for the soldier to drive faster.

Dre tried to speak, R'Mell felt the attempt more than she could hear it. His hand lifted, touching her arm, a silent apology, a silent goodbye, a silent *I tried*. She pressed her forehead to his, her breath shaking.

"I'm sorry, I'm so sorry," she whispered.

Dre's hand slipped from her arm. Romello started to cry.

The world went quiet.

Mell B

Blaque Butterfly Brand Manifesto

We are Blaque Butterfly.

We are born in the shadows but crowned in the sky.
We carry lineage in our wings and purpose in our flight.
We speak softly but shake rooms.
We honor our scars, protect our peace, and rise without permission.

We are cinematic, ancestral, unapologetic.
We build universes from pain and beauty from grit.
We represent every woman who transformed in silence and now moves with power.

We don't escape — we evolve.
We don't whisper — we roar.
We are Blaque Butterfly.

My Why

For a long time, I kept my story locked away because I thought the silence was the only way to survive it. I started this book because I had no other outlet to deal with the weight of my past. When I reached out for help, I found doors closed; I had no one to talk to, and I reached a point where even the specialists no longer wanted to hear my pain.

I realized then that there was no one coming to save me. There was no one to help heal me, but me.

Writing these pages was not a choice made out of creative ambition—it was a necessity for survival. It was the only way to process the traumas that threatened to pull me under. Life dealt me a terrible hand, one that most would have folded on long ago. But I chose to stay at the table. I continued to play the game, not because it was easy, but because I refused to let the hand I was dealt be the end of my story.

If you have ever felt abandoned by the people meant to support you, or if you've had to become your own sanctuary when the world felt cold, I hope these words find you. I didn't write this to relive the breaking; I wrote it to document the rebuilding. This series is proof that even when you are left to heal yourself, you can still find a way to win.

Author Bio – Mell B

Mell B is a bold storyteller, entrepreneur, and visionary creative who writes with fire, truth, and unapologetic power. As the founder of **Butterfly Enterprises, LLC**, she builds brands the same way she builds stories—strategically, fearlessly, and with purpose.

Her debut novel, *Blaque Butterfly*, is a gripping tale of transformation, trauma, loyalty, and revenge—centered on a woman who refuses to stay broken. Mell B doesn't just write about evolution; she embodies it. Her work explores the emotional layers of survival, family bonds, street politics, and the quiet strength of women who rise from ashes and rebuild empires.

Beyond the page, Mell B is the voice behind *Mell B's Morning Kickstart*, where she inspires listeners daily with empowerment, culture, history, and unapologetic truth. Whether through literature, radio, or business, her mission remains the same:

To help others **Emerge. Evolve. Elevate.**

When she isn't creating worlds on paper or building brands, Mell B is expanding her literary universe and developing the next chapter of the Blaque Butterfly saga.

www.ingramcontent.com/pod-product-compliance
Lightning Source LLC
Chambersburg PA
CBHW020636260626
47157CB00008B/2765